DEEP OVERSTOCK

#3: Paranormal Romance
November 2018

" It doesn't matter who you are or what you **"**
look like, so long as somebody loves you.

Road Dahl

ROM - PARANORMAL

EDITORIAL

EDITORS-IN-CHIEF: Bobby Eversmann

MANAGING EDITORS: Ariel Kusby

PROSE: Mickey Collins & Bobby Eversmann

POETRY: Ariel Kusby

SOCIAL MEDIA: Ariel Kusby & Piers Rippey

WEB DESIGN: Robert Eversmann

INTERIOR DESIGN: Mickey Collins

COVER DESIGN: Ariel Kusby

CONTACT: deepoverstock@gmail.com
deepoverstock.com

Letter from the Editors

Beloved Readers,

Thank you for picking up the third issue of Deep Overstock, the booksellers' journal.

In March of 2018, Deep Overstock started as a means to connect and share the creative work of booksellers. So many of our fellow bookstore employees are writers, illustrators, or comic artists. We wanted to give them and ourselves a venue to explore new work - and self-imposed deadlines are good motivators as well.

Within the sexy pages of issue three you'll find content inspired by one of the most overlooked and derided sections in a bookstore: Paranormal Romance. Often tucked away in a dark, smelly aisle like a werewolf's tail tucked between his legs as he asks his beloved for her tentacle in marriage, Paranormal Romance offers a rich field of untapped potential of pleasures of the guiltiest kinds.

You took our ears and put your ancient tongues in them! You took our eyes for blood-vision sacrifice! You stole our hearts and brains from our graves and made new bodies made of air!

We will be forever grateful, palpitating, cursing your very name.

We begged you, 'No! Not furry love!' But oh we've come to love it. We begged you, 'No! Not sex-ghosts from days past!' But, baby, we've got chills all over. 'No! Not Bacteria of Love!' But we're so infected we're levitating above our beds. We begged you, 'Yes, unicorns! Yes, Robert Pattinson!' ...and you gave them to us. Again and again.

In short: We are undeadly graveful for your sexy submissions.

We hope that you will fall in love equally with our next theme, that theme being...

Mater Dei

by Jonathan van Belle

"*Vincere*," she says, "or die."—her first words to me (and her last to me, as I die on my beloved Anacapa Island).

In her grass crown, her red-feather ruff (to match her scarlet teeth), and necklaced with the heads of Dodo, Laughing Owl, and Great Auk, she dances, dances, dances. She dances like Stalingrad and the Somme.

"*Cuncti simus concanentes!*" ("Let us all sing together!")—but she bleats, hisses, growls, moos.

"Why must I dance?"

"*Deo fecunda!—fecunda!*—or die," she neighs.

We had met everywhere; arroyos, the sea cliffs of La Jolla, in vernal pools hid among San Diego mesa mint—we met even in the sepals of the mint. We met every hour; in the eyes of dead crows, in the corners of ceilings, at the bottom of the Lafayette Reservoir.

"*Pugnare!*—or die," she always said, smiling, palms extended, meat cleaver hung from a ring in her nose.

Together we killed bluebucks, red gazelles, the Cathars, the Carthaginians, Gandhi.

"Why do you kill?"

In response, she quoted from Martial's Epigrams: "*Os et labra tibi lingit, Manneia, catellus: non miror, merdas si libet esse cani.*" ("Your little dog licks your lips and mouth, Manneia. No wonder, since a dog likes eating shit.")

"I love you," I said 29,214 times. We mated—mated through the dinosaurs, through their organs, their lizard hips and tongues. We squirreled away their scales in ash and ice. If need be, we mated as maggots. We danced maggot-masked on every continent and island.

She loves power, overpowering, exponentiating powers—maximizing power (thus her grass crown—thus I knew that she would kill me, inhumanely, someday).

I chose Anacapa Island for my death (she let me choose a few of the details). She dressed me in gray hair and liver spots. She built an altar of mushrooms, bound me in rope worms, and laid me on the altar. She reached out her winged left hand with its beaked fingers and they plunged into my eyes, my nostrils, my mouth. I wish I could transfer to you the winding-in, giving-out, distant, derealized sensation of dying (my perfect love has promised me that she'll grant my last wish—for her sake).

"Gloria in excelsis Natura! Vincere!—or die."

Is There Anyone Awake

by Desmond Everest Fuller

Jordan was the youngest guy on the crew that season. Never worked a winter on an offshore rig, and so was more prone to incidents like becoming involved with ghosts.

We all stood, zipped up to the nose, leaning into the bluster of the last helicopter as it whipped the snow falling over the rig and the black chop below. Jordan asked how long till they came back as the Exxon Mobile insignia on the chopper's belly quickly fell up into the dark all around. I don't think anyone said anything. We weren't a talkative bunch.

We heard Jordan see the ghost about a week into the season. I was in my bunk counting down from five thousand. Nick and Alden were playing cards. It was high-pitched, metallic, ringing off everything but what was plastic. A short puncturing scream and then a pause before our boots on the metal floor.

He'd seen her standing on the catwalk just above the stairs going down to the boiler. Hell, I'd get spooked too, high efficiency bulbs casting everything a dull red. We all thought so. But Jordan shook his head with a dog's certainty and kept pointing to the grated metal floor. Right there.

We took him back to the mess and broke out the cards. I was still shaking off the sound of his voice cracking, that scream coming out of somewhere in him you hope you never find in yourself.

Nick sat Jordan down, a hand on his shoulder. "Just jitters, son."

Alden nodded like his head might roll off. "It's like those dog-sledders that run outta Nome, that big race. Every year people are seeing things on the ice in the dark."

"Iditarod," I said.

Alden threw down his cards. A junk hand. "You-did-her-what?"

"That sled race is called The Iditarod. They start seeing things from sensory dep and fatigue."

"Oh," Alden pulled his T-shirt down over his stomach. "Well I'm glad we cleared that up."

"Whuppty-Whup." Nick muttered, glowering into his beard. He'd been holding a straight.

Jordan didn't talk that whole night but to say yes and no and once that the ghost had painted toenails. We all decided to ignore that one.

I didn't ever see anything, working offshore rigs, but my own first winter in Alaska took some adjustment. I couldn't have pictures of my kids in my bunk. I know that now when I sign on for these seasons. We ran our routine checks, played cards and slept in our cabins. The howling ocean on all sides whipped the darkness that stretched beyond the water, like a black lid between us and any thought of a sunrise. Sleep felt like something you were trying to fake until you tricked yourself into dreaming.

I could count my way into sleep, most of the time. I'd count through just about anything that had me twisted up, whatever hurtful memory. Like being a little kid catching a soccer ball in the face, crying out of the blinding pain while everyone called me a sissy, and my dad pulled on my shirtfront, telling me to man-up. That'd go away in 500, 499, 498... But dad's fist full of shirt pulled the string tied to when I was sixteen, the Harney brothers slapping me around, yanking on my collar, stretching out the neck of my new shirt, just being mean cause I was still fat. 495, 494, 493... Mrs. Marsh from the Lutheran church pulled up in her pukemobile, said they should be ashamed, and it seemed like only I caught the shame, my face even redder for an adult to see me like that, 492, 491, 490...

I still haven't found a number big enough to count away from my ex telling my kids that I didn't live with them anymore. It was October. My girl Margo's nose was running, standing in the doorway, my car puttering white exhaust in the driveway. I reached back through the door to take her little jacket off the coat tree, but my ex grabbed it. Not my job anymore, she told me, fitting her little arms through the sleeves. I got so mad, I told Margo that Mommy was dying of cancer. That wasn't true, but I was mad and hateful enough to talk that kind of shit, and I'm stuck with it now, 4867, 4866…

So when I'd hit the flat mouth of zero, staring at the ceiling, I'd get up and walk the decks all around in the guts of the rig. That's how I found Jordan on the catwalk where he saw the ghost.

He wasn't talking to himself or nothing like that, just smiling all sheepish like a blushing kid. I still half-wonder if I didn't almost see him pulling his hand out his pants when I came around the corner, how he startled like I had caught him snooping in his dad's closet.

I showed him my watch; I always set a timer marking how long I'd been awake. It was hard to know out here, without the sun. We were quiet then under the hum of the rig. I didn't ask him about the ghost, he just started telling me how she spoke to him. Told me how she drowned, drifting in the arctic waters. She told him she had a German Sheperd back home that got hit by a logging truck, and she thought when she died, she'd go to wherever he and her grandparents were. Instead she just kept floating out to sea long after her body sank. He said she had curly black hair, all stuck wet to her forehead; he really liked that.

I told him to get some sleep.

Alden and Nick didn't seem concerned when I told them later about Jordan. Nick counted out on his fingers: "Knows his way around a tool box, shows up on time, not dangerous, not my problem."

"He might be goin' a little batshit out here but it's gotta be more entertaining than poker." Alden chuckled, "His ghost's probably a girlfriend he left back wherever he's from."

None of us could recall where that might be. Not sure anyone ever asked.

There was a phone mounted on the wall of the mess room that no one ever used. It had a dial-tone, but who wants to risk that phone bill coming out of their pay-check. It hardly registered, just a beige lump on the wall by the door as you came in.

Then it rang.

We were a few rummy games deep when that dusty rattle fell over us. My watch showed that I was going on thirty hours no sleep. I looked around to see if everyone else heard it too.

Old Nick sheltered his hand like the call was someone peeking on his cards.

Alden put a hand over his heart. "Jesus, I thought that was one of the pumps failing."

After five rings, I got up and answered the damn thing.

A young-sounding guy who talked like he forgot that there was a ringing phone in his hand asked if we'd deliver out of town. Was this Dominoes in Kenai?

I turned and winked at the guys, put the call on speakerphone. I said that, yes, this was Dominoes. I waved their laughter down to the floor and kept going. I even mimed writing down the guy's address. Alden was snorting red. Nick had an eager glint to that pair of ice chips he uses for eyes.

I heard the guy speak away from the phone to someone. A woman's voice in the background. I couldn't make out a damn word in the static. Just the shape of a woman's voice. I realized I didn't know how long I'd gone without talking to a woman.

I took the guy's order and told him we'd have it out to him in about twenty minutes, hung up and went back to playing cards, laughing all round the table. Forty minutes later I was about to drop a pretty solid straight when the phone started harping off the wall. You'd think that he'd've checked the number by then. I leaned against the wall, telling him I was really sorry, but if he'd give me the order again I'd have the driver run it out to him free of charge.

He sighed like I was asking him to file his taxes over again.

"I'll have to ask Jess again, see what the hell she wanted. She'll just change her mind by the time y'all get here anyway."

I scoffed, "Can't know if you're doing right if right's changing every five minutes, am I right?"

He laughed weakly, and that deflated panting sound gave me the idea.

I said, "Let me help you out. Put your lady on the phone. If I take the order straight from her, there's no blaming you when she decides it's not what she wants."

He chewed that. While his peabrain mulled it over, I felt the hot need for something welling up in me. I wanted him to give her that phone, I wanted to hear her voice in my ear. I wanted it badly.

"Yeah?" Jess's voice sounded tired, dredged up from the bottom of the day. I imagined her squinting in the weak electric light over a kitchen sink.

I told her I wanted to know what she wanted. I wanted to hear it from her so I could be sure I got it right. "That guy doesn't seem to be holding it down," I said.

There was a pause before the what's-this-about.

"Your pizza," I murmured.

"Oh, yeah." She drew out her words like smoke. "He'd talked about that. Sorry, I'd forgot."

I asked if she was making it through winter alright.

Barely. The plow broke down two weeks ago, and he'd only just fixed it today. They'd been stuck. Ran out of groceries. She'd tried to thaw a chocolate cake his mother bought them at Kroger's a year ago. It was already baked when they'd tossed it in the freezer, so she ran the tap hot over the plastic bag swaddling the cake. There was a hole in the bag, and black streams of melted frosting bled down the drain, and it became this wet flaky thing that was still in the sink. Took running out of cigarettes to get him off his ass and fix that plow.

"Sorry," Jess said after a long pause, her voice low and grainy. "Weren't we ordering a pizza?"

I told Jess what I wanted. I wanted to be in a bar with wood chairs and the smell of steaks cooking and have a beer with her, maybe break some billiards and put a song on the jukebox. I'd feel safe with all those people around. I wouldn't be thinking about how my ex won't let me see the kids, because everything would be new and clean like the air in some mountain town where we'd find ourselves. Had she ever been to Colorado? I wasn't sure I remembered the sound of birds singing.

I was hunched over the phone. I paused, and she sat with me in the space between us. The hum of the phone line. She told me that I should know: she had a glass eye, a green one, like a marble. People called her a witch so often she wondered if she was really was one. Everything in her life felt cursed.

I told her I didn't care. I just wanted off this tub of metal guts in the middle of nothing but the salt wind that wouldn't shut up and the darkness so big our station lights never seemed like they'd last though the nights. I told her she should call me here again after her man passed out because I'd be awake. I was usually awake.

The phone didn't ring again.

Now, I'm sitting alone in the mess, listening to the drone of the rig, the circular throb of its functions keeping us alive. The phone sits against the wall, dull, inert. I rest my chin on my forearms and squint across the room at it.

I'm the only one awake except maybe Jordan. I found him again, a few days ago, consorting with his drowned spirit. He pointed at the metal grating beneath our feet, crouching down to wipe his fingers across it. Drops of water and the smell of subliming metal.

"That's where she stands," he said.

We stood looking at the blank wall in front of us.

"She asked me to take my clothes off last night," he muttered. "I wanted to, damn I wanted to, but what if you'd come down here like just now? Y'all would lock me in my cabin and call the helicopter to take me away."

He gripped the railing and leaned slowly back and forth. I stood there, unsure.

"Why can't you find your own spot?" he asked before stalking off, leaving me staring down at water drops clinging to the walkway. I stayed a minute, half-hoping a drowned girl would materialize, all wet black hair and round pale cheeks. A succubus I could give over to, a glass eye to hypnotize me. And I was jealous of Jordan, like I needed the haunting more than he did.

I don't walk down by the boiler anymore. When I've finished all my checks and the mess room has cleared out after the last round of Texas-hold'em, I linger in the warm drone alone, the others worming their way into sleep. I've stopped keeping track of how long I've been awake. There's no number to count down from anymore. Sometimes I get up and hold the phone to my ear, drifting in the dial tone. I fold my elbows on the table and press my eyes into my forearms till there are colors swimming in the dark. Down there I'll hear the phone ringing, and find someone breathing on the other end, about to tell me what's next.

Ghost Hotel

by Ariel Kusby

If I summoned you into my chest I'd let the poltergeist pulse through muscle.

•

If I could summon you into a deep yard, under an unbuttoning moon, I'd never stop summoning you.

•

I'd summon you silken and night-velvet, safe vapor like shower steam, like a hot spring pink body, dressed up in a wet summoning.

•

I summon that invisibility now with a spell that hangs silent in the air, like a ghost story I hold in my room with fake walls, a hexing cry muffled at midnight.

•

I will always be summoning you into any empty room.

•

I am summoning your black root and glitter, your odor amongst the litter of plums out back.

•

You are summoned black and blossoming to my night garden.

•

I summon you to enjoy your stay.

•

Mostly you are summoned pale as your form demands, white as the teeth that hold you, white as my bones like wands that will never stop summoning you.

The Tribe of Amalfia

by Michael Calkins

"'The Tribe of Amalfia welcomes all shifters in the central Ohio area to an evening of community and sensuality.' What a load of crap. I mean, I been here three hours now and I ain't had one second of sensuality. And the only community I had is talking to you, no offense. It's been real nice to meet you."

"I'm pretty new to the area and I been starting to feel pretty horny, so I thought this would be a great chance to meet some others like us and maybe get laid. I mean, back where I come from all the shifters I knew were always looking to get some, you know."

"Billings. In Montana. There weren't a lot in town. Most of them spent their time living in the woods, you know, literally like animals. But they'd get jonesing for some beer or weed and they'd come in town and we'd get together. It was always a wild time. You had to really try not to get your rocks off. I always liked to do it full wild. It just don't feel as good when I'm hybrid for some reason."

"Oh, sorry. Panther. Long and sleek. The ladies go nuts. Even if they don't want to fuck they can't keep their hands off the fur. And you're, what, a deer?"

"Elk, sorry. You'd think I'd know better. Can't say I've ever been with a deer, or elk, or whatever. Kinda strange, given where I'm from. Course, I think all of them I ever saw was dudes and I just ain't into doing it with dudes. Not that I got a problem if that's what others like. To each his damn own, I say."

"I ain't had any tonight, to answer your question, because of a certain red fox who can't keep her mouth shut. See, I said I didn't know anybody in the area, but it turns out I met this red fox back in Billings and she's here tonight. And she must have seen me before I saw her and she's been going around talking shit about me to all the ladies. And thanks to that I couldn't get any of them to get with me."

"No, I don't mind telling you. It's no big deal, but she's making it one. See, we only did it once and I guess she didn't like it too much 'cause, well, cats have got barbs on their dicks."

"Jeezus, man, what are you making that face for? We don't got spikes on there. Just barbs. They ain't sharp or nothing. They're just these firm little bumps. For extra stimulation. I mean, if cat dicks was tearing up the insides of cat pussies cats would just go extinct, you know. And I know not everybody I been with has liked it, but this red bitch is going around making it sound like my dick's gonna get caught on their cervix or something. Everybody's been avoiding me, 'cept George."

"He's the chimp over there. Talking to the red fox, as a matter of fact. He come up to me talking about how he just heard about what cats are like and well …. Only like I said before, I ain't interested in dudes that way. And look at that. They're making out. What the fuck? What's the point? I mean, how hard can it be to find a short, bald, hairy-backed old man to fuck?"

"Thanks, man, but it ain't worth staying for another beer. I'm just gonna go. There's a group of Furries that get together once a month at the airport Ramada. If I go in hybrid form I can pass good enough to get in tonight. I don't love going hybrid, but there's a cute gray squirrel I've seen there that I'd like to know better."

"You have a good night."

Tips for Dating the Minotaur
by Stephen Kelly

When kissing the Minotaur, get a firm grip on his horns

> It's your best chance to avoid a concussion

Make plenty of noise when you enter the labyrinth

> You don't want to surprise the Minotaur

> But don't whistle

> He hates whistling

The Minotaur likes oats

> Also, scrambled eggs

> Also, the brains of heroes he vanquishes

You can never flatter the Minotaur enough

> But don't ever, ever look at his snout

> Or ask about his mom

Don't chew gum

> The Minotaur will think you're making fun of him

And don't turn your back on the Minotaur

> This may invite a charge

When uncertain, treat the Minotaur as you would a toddler

> Holding a stick of dynamite

> > In one hand

And a match

In the other

Flowers work, sometimes

And always bring a ball of string to find your way out

Whatever you do, don't tug on the Minotaur's tail

No matter how many times he asks you

Ghostfuckers

by Kellye McBride

We, and by "we" I mean Ghostfuckers, are a paranormal organization started by me, a part-time gym teacher and my cousin Jerry, a full-time manager at Bob's Big Boy, who came together for one mission and one mission only: to fuck ghosts. Why ghosts, you ask? There is nothing wrong or shameful about being attracted to disembodied spirits. Or dead people for that matter. We're just like you, normal people with a passion and purpose. That's why we created this group in the first place, to seek out other like-minded individuals who don't mind getting it on with poltergeists.

Don't get me wrong, seducing ghosts is serious business: you have to create the right conditions or they won't even show up. Just ask my cousin Jerry, who spent three hours in an abandoned sawmill with his pants down with only a frostbitten erection to show for it. You got to set the right mood, scatter some rose petals, light some candles. Ask them about their day. Maybe work in a foot massage, if they're the type of spirit with feet, for example. Ghosts have all the time in the world (they're dead, remember?) so they don't like to be rushed. Don't skip foreplay, and whatever you do, don't bring up the subject of their untimely demise. I've found it to be a turn off with the recently deceased.

Here are a handful of tips I've found to be productive when trying to initiate relations with those who have crossed over to the other side:

Tip One: Learn to embrace your dark side

Ghosts love it when you play up your own inner turmoil because it makes them feel better about themselves. We've all heard the stories about how ghosts usually can't pass over because of some "unfinished business," and I'm here to tell you that your suspicions are correct. All ghosts have their insecurities, just like people. So what better way of establishing a connection with them then revealing yours? Maybe read some of your terrible poetry from your high school diary or perform an uncomfortable jazz trumpet solo. They might find your awkwardness endearing and thus be more willing to possess you.

Tip Two: Plan ahead

Remember, you are entering the ghost's home turf. Chances are they are more comfortable with the area they are haunting than you are so be sure to look out for booby traps. Again, just ask my cousin Jerry who once got kicked in the nuts by a rigged suit of armor. Arrive before sundown with a comfortable sleeping bag, EMF detector, and plenty of snacks. You might want to think twice before video recording your experience, however. Some ghosts are a little camera shy, so remember to ask and be respectful. You don't want to have an angry spectre on your hands if they find out they've accidentally been videotaped. Pack clean underwear and cologne. Practice good grooming habits because it lets them know you care, even if they no longer have a sense of smell.

Tip Three: Set the stage for romance

Ghosts are shy when it comes to initiating things. That's why it's on you to make them as comfortable as possible (see Tip One). Scream a little. Rattle a few chains. Maybe draw something on the walls in blood. Personally, I like to indulge in a little throat singing or Gregorian chants while I limber up. Drives the ghost ladies wild. My ex-wife Linda always tells me that if I put as much effort into seducing ghosts as I did in our marriage, we might still be together. I say nonsense. Ghost women never bug you about the little things, like quitting your job to pursue puppeteering full time or investing in all of your shared savings in Bitcoin.

Tip Four: Prepare your body

When your ghost lover finally possesses you, you might be out for hours. Possibly even days. In that time, you need to take the appropriate precautions. Hydration is an essential part of any paranormal seduction.

Here's how to make your own spectral smoothie, guaranteed to restore your electrolytes after sweet, phantasmic lovemaking:

1 part baby formula

2 parts Gatorade

1 banana, for potassium

Chia seeds

Crushed ice, to serve

As always, check with your doctor to make sure that you can handle the stress. Get your heart and blood pressure checked out or schedule a routine physical beforehand.

Tip Five: Have fun and be yourself

Some people take their attraction to spirits very, very seriously, but I also think it's important to just have fun with it. A sense of humor is key when trying to attract the right kind of ghost. You have to be willing to laugh at yourself. Got a tiny dick or flabby vagina? Make jokes about it constantly to demonstrate how un-self-conscious about it you are. Got a weird mole on your ass? Get a giant neck tattoo to distract them from it. Have you recently moved back in with your parents after a soul crushing divorce? See if they would be willing to sublet.

Tip Six: Make sure you are not interrupted by another paranormal investigation team

I don't know how many times I've been in the middle of a lovemaking session and been rudely interrupted by another team of paranormal investigators who booked the same haunted location at the same time. I cannot stress the importance of securing your location early and in advance. Case in point: my cousin Jerry was at the Trans-Allegheny Lunatic Asylum the same night they were shooting an episode of *Ghost Hunters*, and, well, long story short he was almost filmed bare-assed on national television. The folks over at the Lewis County Sherriff's Department thought he was on LSD and locked him up in the drunk tank. We shouldn't have to explain our desires to everyone (Linda), this is America. Our forefathers didn't die for our freedoms only to have their descendants face this kind of discrimination.

Tip Seven: Spice things up with a little pillow talk

The trick to maintaining relations with your ghost lover and keep things interesting is routinely engaging in a little naughty dialogue. Say things like, "This cold spot is making me hard" or, "You look so sexy inside that floating bedpan." Seducing the paranormal doesn't give you license to be boring, let your inhibitions go and your sexuality run free! A word on engaging multiple spirits: Ghosts tend to be a little bit possessive (no pun intended) of their hosts, so I would make sure that it is alright with your primary spirit before initiating contact with any others, simultaneously or otherwise. Poor cousin Jerry found himself in a nightmare ordeal last year when he was possessed by Lizzie Borden's sister and nearly got his tackle box lopped off by Lizzie herself! Ho ho! Nearly gave him thirty whacks, and not the dirty kind!

Tip Eight: Set aside your assets

You might think that seducing ghosts would be less expensive than regular dating: no flowers, dinners, or jewelry to buy. But you would be wrong. I've drained the remainder of my savings into traveling across the country with my cousin Jerry after the divorce. The money tended to go rather quickly after deducting the following expenses: giant neck tattoo, Chia seeds, rabies vaccine, puppeteering lessons, a dozen penis braces, bedpan, EMF equipment, and bail for cousin Jerry. Therefore, it's a good idea to make sure that your assets are in order, should you decide to embark on a haunted sexual odyssey like me. The paranormal playboy lifestyle is not intended for everyone, believe me. You'll have to make some sacrifices, financial or otherwise, along the way. Some people (Linda) might not understand your decisions, but that doesn't make them any less valid. So I would encourage you all to get out there and embrace the beauty of the unknown! Hump a headless horseman! Bang a banshee! Diddle a demon! The world is yours!

The Woman with a Thousand Heads #18

by Glen Armstrong

Oh, crazy speech, liberated

from the cause itself!

Oh, human clamshell still

slippery with the grease of sex!

Oh, heaven-bound ephemera

above our houses like space junk

built from a much needed

summer rain! Oh, telltale

stain on the soul!

Oh, ghost of Otis Redding!

Oh, cheese course! Oh, secret

underpants or lack thereof!

Oh, breath and bardic convention!

Rise! Rise! Rise! Rise! Rise!

?
IF PEOPLE CANNOT SEE ME...
DO I REALLY EXIST?

BY OAKTEA

*

OAKTEAPARTY ON INSTAGRAM, TWITTER, TWITCH AND TUMBLR

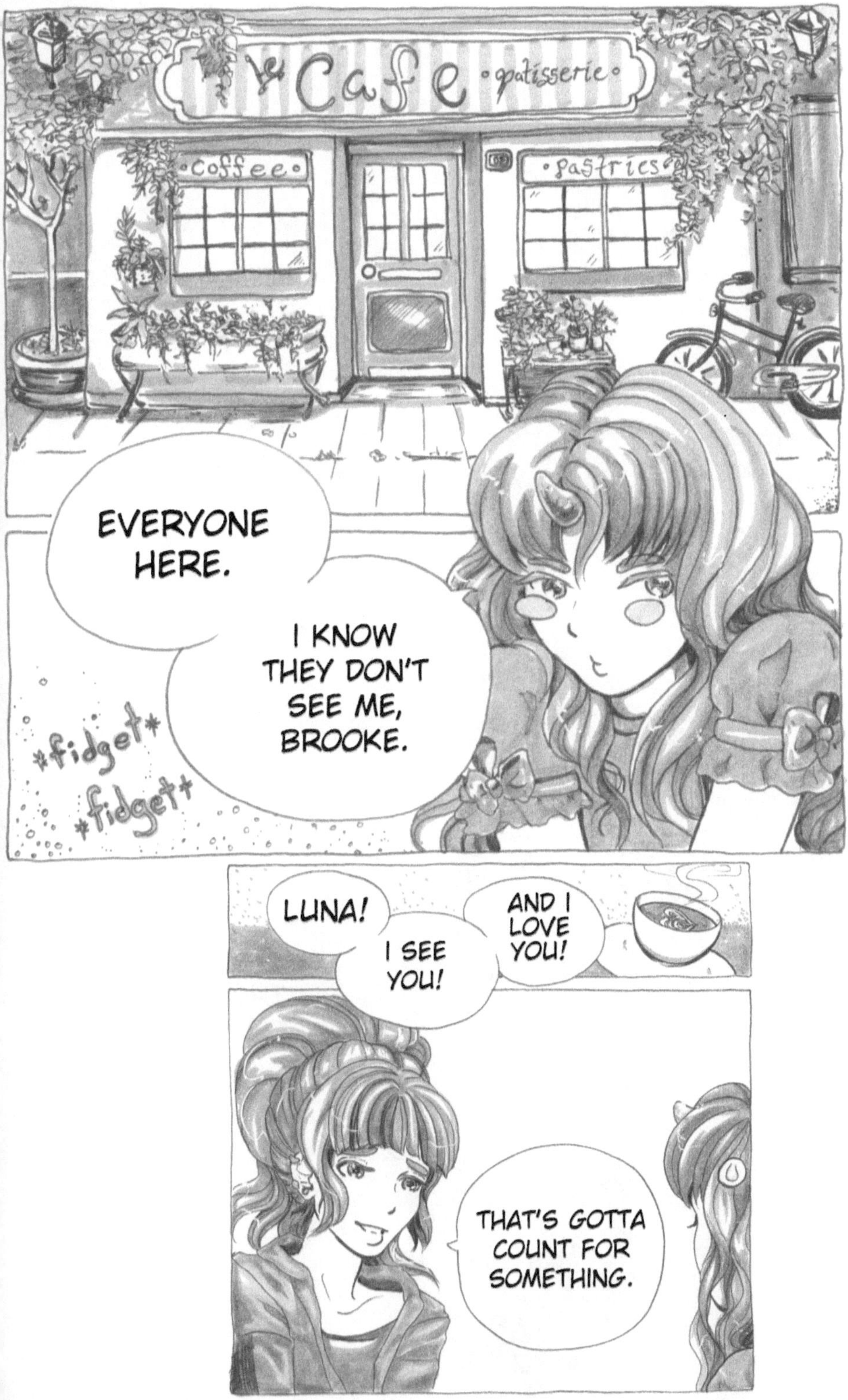

EVERYONE HERE.
I KNOW THEY DON'T SEE ME, BROOKE.
fidget
fidget
LUNA!
I SEE YOU!
AND I LOVE YOU!
THAT'S GOTTA COUNT FOR SOMETHING.

BUT IT DOES CAUSE PROBLEMS.
LIKE HERE!
THEY ONLY GAVE US ONE FORK!

WELL THEN...
WE CAN SHARE WHAT WE HAVE.
IT DOESN'T HAVE TO BE MINE.

LUNA!
I HAVE A SURPRISE FOR YOU!
gasp
THEY'RE SO PRETTY!
THANK YOU!

YOU KNOW...
I WOULD DO ANYTHING FOR YOU.
COME-
THERE'S MORE!

THERE ARE UNICORNS EVERYWHERE!

AND THEY SEE ME!!!

THIS IS THE BEST GIFT!

I WOULD DO ANYTHING FOR YOU.

AND ALL YOU NEEDED

WAS TO BE SEEN.

I NEEDED YOU TO BE SEEN, TOO.

I WANT THE WORLD TO KNOW

HOW AMAZING YOU ARE.

The Pitcher Plant

by Cosima Bee Concordia

I'm short on rent so I call Daddy. His phone rings five times before it goes to voicemail, but I end it before it beeps to record. I always call him instead of texting because he has a shitty old flip phone that he pecks at with his pointer finger while he squints. I make fun of him for it often, although it's a sore spot for him and it sometimes gets me in trouble.

He has several times and not-so-jokingly referred to himself as Daddy Warbucks, which I guess is appropriate given our arrangement. He has a head of luxurious brown hair, but insists he'd shave to it full on gleaming bald if he was less self-conscious about the bumpy shape of his head. I find it a little endearing that he's willing be vulnerable around me, but I'm mostly just glad he's too insecure to get rid of my handholds for when his cock is plunged into my guts. The weird thing is that he must be at least a little bit delusional, because when I feel the scalp under all that hair it feels like the top half of a gigantic polished marble.

The phone's ringing, and it's him. I answer and tilt my voice up like a see-saw.

Hiiiiii Daddy.

Hey, I saw that you called, he says in a voice that's…moderate I guess? Kind of average and a bit monotone, obviously masculine but not like that deep or anything. Then: Why didn't you leave a voicemail?

I sigh. Daddy has a thing about voicemails, like there's some obligation to them, like why would you call if you're not going to leave one? I don't do them because I mean who does voicemail anymore, but also because I don't like my voice, or at least I used to dislike my voice and now I do out of habit. Now I like my voice enough when I'm speaking, but I mean, basically no one likes their voice when they're recorded right? A few years ago there was another guy who had offered to do a video with me for a bunch of money, even showed me this whole set up of expensive cameras, but then he gave me a script to read over because I had my own lines and when he said it was a deal-breaker I just shook my head and was out of there. I've skipped over a lot of lines most girls would swear up and down that they'd never cross, but letting my voice be forever trapped on the internet is my hard limit.

I bite the bottom of my lip a bit while apologizing to get the tone right, and then take my time telling him just how much I miss him since last week and how good he made me feel while in that round about sideways kind of way mentioning that my dumb landlord raised the rent again, that big mean man taking advantage of little ol' me. It's not long until he starts to stumble over his words and says he wants to come over.

Of course Daddy, I simper. Why do you think I called?

I wait a while because Daddy lives on the other side of town, one of those areas they call historic because the houses are old and pretty and have rich people in them. I've always assumed his house is unreasonably big, like the kind of space you would only ever need in order to keep buying more beautiful, expensive things. I bet he has a big grand piano or something that barely ever gets played, just sitting there to look fancy.

At the end of the call, he said he wanted to do the full weekend together and asked if it's okay because it's something that we haven't done before. I said it sounds lovely, and suggested a picnic where he could discreetly fuck me against a tree or in the field among some fancy cheese and pickle plates, and he didn't protest. If he wants me for that long he's likely planning something nice, and I'm more than willing to make it worth his while.

I stand in front of the mirror and pucker my lips. I've been told many times over the years that guys prefer girls without makeup, their accidental subtext being that they prefer us to have all of the subtle groundwork to look like a just-woke-up-model while leaving out all distinguishing personality and flair. I reapply my #71 Seashell Rose and smooth the uneven bottom left edge with my pinky nail— turning my head slightly to both sides to admire my curled ink-black lashes, masterwork eyebrows, contoured cheekbones, and glowing fairy skin. Men that think women put on makeup just for them are truly tragic.

The bed has been made, fitted sheet tucked in and pastel pink pillows arranged just so with my extra-large plushy of Appa the Sky Bison propped by the headboard in such a way that he stares into your soul. I light candles that smell like cinnamon, and check in my side table drawer to make sure my switch blade is where it's supposed to be. My on-again off-again girlfriend slash best friend Ivy gave me both the knife and Sky Bison at once—the blade to protect myself and Appa to watch over me. She had squeezed my hand so hard that it fell asleep, staring me down with those huge green eyes while lecturing me about my supposed death wish, making me promise to be more cautious.

And she's right—I have had some close calls where all of the worst things could have come to pass, situations that lucky me has come away from only having suffered loud slurs and some violent threats and maybe a push or two. Out of my friends, I'm the one who's always doing the thing that seems stupid afterward, so maybe there is something fucked up about how I make my decisions. It's not like I want to die or anything though— I've just accepted the reality of being a Girl Like Me in a world like this one.

I pick up the switch blade and flip it open. The handle is a textured honey but the blade is gnarly, like the kind you could just firmly disembowel someone with in a single go. I've never been much of a fighter, and deep down I think that if someone really wants to do me in and my only choice is to stab them I'd probably just let them get it over with. That being said, I suppose it's never bad to have more choices rather than less.

Ever since I was able to give up my other clients for Daddy alone, I've been inconsistent about taking precautions because I don't feel like he's going to randomly attack me after paying me allowance for months, but Ivy's been back on me. I slip my knife back into the side table and I text her my plan (he's coming over tonight and sleeping over, activities until, assumedly, Sunday evening) followed by emojis of a dancing woman, an egg plant, and some thirsty looking raindrops. A few minutes later, she texts back Have fun and BE CAREFUL! followed by a classic big red heart.

Soon afterward, the doorbell buzzes and I run to the door to let Daddy in. He's dressed a little too business-y for my taste but he still looks handsome, especially because of his five o' clock shadow that I like in a kind of masochistic way. He's holding a bouquet of what he says are dahlias, these giant red flaming things that remind me of imploding stars on the Nature channel, and a navy blue overnight bag. I giggle and thank him and say come on in and make yourself comfortable, I'm just going to find a vase for these flowers, which really means I'm going to find my one water pitcher and that's going to work fine.

When I get back, he's sitting on a chair in my tiny living room, stiffly perched on the edge like a bird. I hunch down my eyebrows and smile, moving toward him in the same way I would playing with a toddler or a dog. Hey gloomy, what's got you looking so doomy? I say in sing-song, pushing him backwards into his chair and loosening his tie. Then he's grabbing my hair with his left hand and pulling me in and up with the other, and I'm being carried, damsel like, into my bedroom.

A few times I've called myself a whore in front of him by accident and each time he'd get all quiet and concerned, like I'm about to throw myself off a bridge or something. He'd stroke my cheek, tell me that I'm beautiful, and go on about how I shouldn't say mean things about myself. Every time I'm tempted roll my eyes and launch into how there's nothing mean about it or about how we're out here reclaiming it or just say like You know what words are right? But instead I stop myself and smile and stroke his cheek back and say Thanks Daddy, because in the end that's part of why I'm here, the role I've been brought in to play. He just wants to be the wealthy Daddy who wipes away the smudge of poverty from this poor little orphan girl with his fistfuls of cash, and I let him.

One night I had a dream and he's standing over me, wailing Out, damned spot! like Lady MacBeth, furiously rubbing his bloodied hands together as crisp hundred dollar bills rain down on my naked body to cleanse my dirty soul. I think I may have cum a little before waking up.

Just for the record, I'm not actually an orphan, or at least not in the sense that my parents are dead, although I've internalized the fantasy pretty thoroughly and guess it's metaphorically true enough for me to not feel too bad about keeping up the ruse. If it means anything, I was never the first to slam the front door after saying You're dead to me, or to scream Get out of my house after melodramatically opining how Our son is dead.

The thing about being dead to someone but still being alive is that they effectively get to be dead back. That's what being dead is really about—kind of being preserved in that place that you were when you were first declared dead in everyone's minds, like a picture that's just a little bit haunted. You know, the ones whose eyes follow you when you walk by. So I guess what I'm trying to say is that that's what my parents are: these fixed images that sometimes replay little sound bites of what they said before we were dead to each other. I get nostalgic for it sometimes, even knowing that time fucks up memory faster than a nail in a Coke can. None of the things I miss are all the way real.

If you didn't know, cis guys think about the size of their cocks a lot, and before Daddy I sorted my clients, with relative success, into three separate camps with that fact in mind. The first, and probably most common, were always sure to mention that their cock was the biggest and best of the whole lot. I would always make sure to match even their grossest exaggerations with enthusiastic support, because in the end what they fetishize more than anything else is for you to fetishize wanting it. Even when it came to those who could sort of back up their porn-y texts about horse-like proportions didn't necessarily have any idea what to do with it other than lay on top of me and thrust. I have toys that size that don't tire themselves out right when things are getting good. Plus, flesh and blood dicks don't vibrate.

The second camp are usually concerned about their own inadequacy, sending me pics and playing the game of What do you think? with the expectation that I am a kind god offering salvation. And so I tell them Yes, of course baby, because all they want to be told is that their cock is Good with a capital G, just as it was meant to be. Although there are intersections between these two camps, the biggest difference may be that Camp 2 constantly must be reassured that they lasted a long time or that they were really hard enough, whereas Camp 1 merely assumes this as truth.

Being a Girl Like Me adds even more credibility to my testimony in the eyes of both these groups, as they get to look at my genitals for comparison—finding reassurance that they could never imagine purposefully softening and shrinking or doing away with it entirely. In addition, I carefully omit that it's been primarily people without functioning penises that have given me the best orgasms of my life, for fear of wounded egos and the violence that could evaporate up from them—two phenomena almost as closely linked as steam from a tea kettle.

Camp 3 is still largely phallocentric, but regardless of size it's about stepping on their sense of self a bit instead of building them up. This can come in many forms—treating me like a goddess and serving me, giving me their money, licking my boots, etcetera etcetera. Of course the pinnacle of all of this is feminization—because what could be more degrading and corrosive to your manhood than being made—or in many of their cases forced—to wear a little bit of makeup and a dress? I suppose that's one way to put the service I offered: sparing them from the unmanly implications of their own free will.

Some of the sweeter clients want the simplest things once I've gotten them femmed up: someone to brush their hair, to cuddle them in bed, or to exchange fluttery butterfly kisses. Times like that I really started to feel more responsibility for them than I actually had—these souls that just want to be held and feel pretty—because who knows how many among them were repressed trans girls or queer boys or people who are neither, that may never find the space to find out. As the Girl Like Me that they sought out, I'd like to think that I gave each of them a brief respite from their wells of loneliness, and maybe even planted the seed that, if they look hard enough, there's always an escape hatch somewhere.

I only bring all of this to give some context for Daddy and his cock, to point out how unusual it is that's he so utterly unconcerned with it. That's not to say that he doesn't use it, but that he follows none of the patterns of my three camps: no braggadocio, no insecurity, no emasculation. Then I suppose you could say that all of my experiences with cis men have been clients and that they are seeking out sex work specifically because they have a void to fill—that there are plenty of dudes the world over who got over their penis issues in their youth and are now one hundred percent well-adjusted.

In response, I'd say that—beyond my doubts that anyone could ever be well-adjusted—the very idea that Daddy ever went through such a period of masculine adjustment is hard for me to imagine, or, for that matter, even the idea that he ever had a youth at all.

I've never been a huge fan of romance novels, but I can't deny that when we're in the heat of it Daddy certainly makes me feel like I'm in one. He lets be the girl who comes from nothing without anything special going for her who is mysteriously chosen by a rich, successful, and handsome older man. And I think maybe that's how he fucks me like he does: like someone with taste who has chosen to taste me, and who has paid a high price for the privilege. It kind of makes me want to gag a little, but the bills get payed and I cum hard every time.

That's what puts me here, lying on the bed, naked and glistening with sweat, staring up at a whirring ceiling fan in a brain fucked afterglow. I'm not sure where Daddy went but I don't think I care, content in my stillness, when something drops next to my head. Then he's suddenly above me.

I have a surprise for you, he says, his smile all straight white teeth.

I blink my eyes and push myself up on an elbow. Hey, what's this Daddy?

Just open it.

He gestures at his overnight bag he dropped by my head. If you say so Daddy. I heft it up and unzip it while looking at him with one finger to my head and wrinkling my forehead like I'm thinking hard. Ooh, I wonder what it could be? I heft it up and flip it over, and its contents come spilling out. I toss the deflated bag to the side while my jaw drops so close the ground that I probably look like a cartoon.

In front of me are roll upon roll of cash, thick and bound, and, holy shit, all hundreds. Like thousands upon thousands, more money than I've ever seen or handled, the type of money that can change a life permanently. Immediately my mind flashes to an image of a room in a house, and sitting on a chair inside is

Ivy, my head in her lap and a black cat—our cat—sprawled on the top of the couch parallel. She's stroking my hair.

I snap out of it, and look back up into his wide-eyed stare. Um, Daddy? Is this really for me?

You know, you do call me Daddy Warbucks. He grabs my chin with a cupped hand and kisses me hard on the lips. It is, as long as you agree to do one thing for me. He gets on his knees on the floor so he is eye-level and says, There's something different about me that I don't share often, something wonderful, but it is not for everybody. Sometimes people are too scared when they see something new, and will run away. Will you run away?

I find myself judging my reaction time to my bedside table against his, my mind spinning around what's about to go down, but then I look back at the heaping pile of cash. Why would he bring the money if he was just going to off me, and why now? If he just wants some weird sex thing he wildly overestimated the necessary price needed to get me hooked, but it's not like I'm complaining.

I take a deep breath and try to make my smile as authentic as possible. Of course not Daddy! Why would I do a silly thing like that?

Okay. Then here's my secret, he says with complete seriousness. I have a hinge that allows for—for my mouth to get much bigger than usual. And when the hinge swings open, others can come inside me and then—they can see through my eyes, feel what I feel—we can be closer than you could ever imagine. When I open it, I need you to keep your clothes on and step in feet first, until you have slid all of the way in. Then you can leave the rest to me, understand?

My face has been growing more and more disturbed as this this weirdo makes it clear he thinks he can accomplish some IRL vore on me, but then again, maybe this is his strange version of a prank, or, best case, using this as some very roundabout way to ask if he can choke on my foot. So I say Understood, my voice as small and high as a star-struck student having their worldview blown to smithereens.

Good. If you are willing, I'm sure you'll love it. He raises the hands to the side of his face. Once I have opened the hatch, I will not be able to talk until I have closed you inside me.

Yes, Daddy.

His fingers press into his temples, and then begin to turn like a knob.

What happens is that his mouth just—expands. Like his jaw gets lower and his skin becomes stretchy and elastic—like ghostly pale—getting bigger and bigger until his teeth look comically small on the bottom and top, with that little thing that swings at the back of your throat right behind like a little pinkish raindrop. Past the gateway of his mouth, a meaty abyss has opened up, squirming and throbbing in the dark.

I feel like bolting and throwing up and crying all at once, but as I take short breaths I think about how this is exactly what he told me, that this is what he asked, that he had warned me and I had said yes like an idiot. And you could chalk it up to a broken brain or shock or trash parents or whatever you want, but I edge my feet off the bed like a little kid afraid to go down the water slide, inch by inch until they are dangling into the void. Then, all at once the rest of me follows, slipping straight down as the flesh closes in around me and the lights go out.

It's hard to tell exactly how long I'm asleep. Or not asleep— not really. Just not fully there, in the pitch black, floating in meat. I can hear the pump of his blood as the body pulses around me. I wonder if this is what it was like to be in the womb. I wonder if I'm dead.

Unexpectedly, I start to see again. I'm in a huge bed with silky ivory-colored sheets, and it smells like clean laundry. I'm pulling the covers off and getting up, when someone yawns behind me, and I turn around to see a middle-aged woman looking at me, blonde hair across her face. Where you going baby? she says, voice rocky from sleep.

I don't know what to say but I find myself responding: I'm just going to take Zeus for a walk, but I'll be back soon and I'll check in on the kids before I head out. I'm slipping on jeans and a t-shirt and call Come on Zeus, and from his dog bed in the corner a pretty husky rises up out of his bed and does a big dog stretch, before following me as I walk through the door.

My mind whirs as I walk down the hall, the walls covered in pictures of people that don't stay long enough in my vision to see. That voice that had come out of my mouth was manly and monotone—nothing like mine. Is this a dream? I open up a door into a room with dark blue walls and look onto the top bunk of the bunk bed, where a hump rises up and down underneath the covers, before closing the door quietly. Then onto the next room: this one a cheerful pink. I know just where to look here too, a hump on the bed with the purple princess blankets. Zeus follows patiently at my heels.

The house is huge, but I know exactly where to go—down the curled stairs and through the big parlor room and the grand piano, to the front door where Zeus sits and I attach his leash. Then we're outside, and the weather is in that perfect place that it sometimes is in the mornings on really hot days, where everything is just right with a slight breeze and no one's out yet and—

Do you want to say something? I say. I said, do you want to say something? I'm still walking and Zeus trots along by my side just like the good boy he is. This is Daddy, I say, And I'm telling you that I'm giving you the chance to speak.

Everything stops, or I stop, or my reality seems to stop, but I am still walking, and it is clear that I am not dreaming. It is not me that is walking, it is Daddy. Daddy with the mouth, the gaping mouth where I am, the place where I'm trapped, on all sides, suffocating. But here I am, seeing the sidewalk in front of me, the sidewalk surrounded by these gorgeous old houses, the smell of trees and morning and crisp air. So I speak: What is happening? and for the first time really hear my voice, Daddy's voice that is in no way my voice, and a cold wave fills me up, a dread that washes up my spine, suddenly drowning in a tide that I have only felt splashes of for years. What is happening?

And Daddy replies: You're inside me, like I told you. And now you get to be with me, to see what I see, and feel what I feel.

Daddy please, you have to let me out. I can't stand this anymore. I can't stand it, I plead, my desperation sounding unnatural in his voice.

Don't worry, you'll find that it gets easier as time passes, it just takes some time to adjust. Pretty soon you won't even know the difference.

But tomorrow—tomorrow, you said that I would be with you only for the weekend, right? So tomorrow you'll take me home, because the money right?

Sure, tomorrow. Right. Tomorrow, if that's what you want.

I let a few moments pass before I begin screaming Help as loud at the top of his lungs, a bellowing cry that lasts for only moments before his mouth snaps shut and I become voiceless.

We have stopped walking, and Zeus sits and looks up at us. The first rule, he says through clenched teeth, Is that you behave. I am the captain and you are only a passenger. Your sight, your voice, your touch—they are privileges that I can and will revoke at any time. I could ground you and put you back in the dark right now, and you should be thankful for every moment that I don't. Do you understand?

Daddy I—

Are you thankful?

Yes, I—

Say thank you.

Th-thank you Daddy.

Now are you going to behave?

Yes, Daddy.

Good girl.

Neither of us talk again, and we complete the rest of the walk in silence.

I don't know how to explain it—the feeling of doing things and knowing you did that thing while also somehow knowing you're not the one pulling the strings. I want to think it's me going through this day, playing with my kids, kissing my wife, throwing sticks for the dog, reading the newspaper. When I look at his perfectly girly girl and super boy I think about the queer drama kid I was, and how much better off these kids are: how well suited they both are for the world they're training for—princesses and fucking heroes. And wouldn't it be so easy to just take my hands off the wheel and go on autopilot—slip into it like some sort of trance and just drift away? That feeling of revulsion as we look in the mirror and shave his beard could stop—I could just…stop. Disassociate just like I used to, but this time just let the part that is me dissipate like some bad trip.

At dinner, my wife has made us all a delicious lasagna, and it's so good that I take a second big square after the I finish off the first. My daughter looks at me and giggles. Daddy, you eat so much!

That's…because…I'm…a…MONSTER! I roar, fingers bent into claws, pretending to eat her arm as she laughs hysterically.

In this house, we go to sleep early, and a few hours later the lights are off and we're in bed, eyes closed. I can feel my hands beneath the sheets, the silkiness just barely touching down on them. Then something different happens: I'm gone, or, I guess, Daddy is gone but I'm left behind, and with both hands I grab as much of the sheet as I can in clenched fists as the moment passes and I'm pulled down too.

It is dark here, but it is not the same—this is a bigger darkness. I hear voices like bubbles popping all around me, faint and brief but coming from all directions. I don't know how to get to them, but I'm also not sure how to move. They're getting louder, and now I am sure they are women. They are crying but enraged, cowering and begging for their lives but fighting with their claws bared. And don't know how I know but I know that they are like me, girls like me. But they are disappearing—there is meat all around them and there is no one to hear their voices, and they dissolve, melting into the flesh until their voices grow fainter again. And then there are no voices except mine, screaming Come back, don't leave me! But I don't think anyone can hear me. I think maybe I am fading too.

I start to see again. I am already out of bed, outside, Zeus beside us. It is colder this morning, a mist obscuring the street, and the dream starts to come back as I walk. As we walk—no, as he walks. That the part of me that is me, the part encased in this thing I am looking out of—she had a dream, and in it I saw what would happen, or what was already happening. What had happened before, and would happen again.

What a fucked up way to go.

Good morning Daddy, I say, finding that he has allowed me access to his mouth.

I thought I felt you there waking up, he says, more upbeat than I've ever heard him. Good morning sleepy head. How did you enjoy your day yesterday?

It was…it was interesting.

Interesting? You got a taste of my life, of the life you can now experience.

But, I thought you were going to take me back home today, I say, already knowing the answer.

I think—I think we have other plans today.

I take a deep breath, and feel his lungs expand. Why do you do this to us?

To us? Who's us?

To me, to them. To all of the girls you've—I heard them. And I know what's happening, and you need to let me go.

We're still walking, but faster now, his arms swinging from side to side and Zeus keeping perfect pace. Already you are happier than you were yesterday, more accepting as I let you have the life that you could have had—that you were meant to have but squandered, he says, gritting his teeth. And if you heard the voices of the others—it's proof, right?

We both stop talking for a moment as he picks up speed, Zeus loping beside us.

To be honest, I say in between breaths, I'm sorry I asked. I'd rather I was tricked into being eaten by a Tiger or something rather than whatever the fuck you are.

You—all of you—are so disrespectful, never taking even a moment to thank me, never recognizing all the things I do for you.

You need to let me out, people will be looking for me.

People will be looking for you? Your own parents have disowned you because you're a degenerate freak, he laughs. You're a whore. No one will be looking for you.

You're wrong—there are people who care about me, and they know about us. I've given them all of the information and they're expecting me back home tonight.

And you're a fucking liar, he hisses.

I'll forget everything, and no one will ever know. I'll go back home and you'll never hear of me ever again.

He's silent.

They have your photo.

What? We have stopped as he bends his knees to breathe, back and forehead slick with sweat.

Your photo. I took it on my phone while you were sleeping. They know what you look like. They'll find that photo when I don't show up tomorrow, and then they'll find you. And your perfect little life will be ruined.

No one will believe your little friend whores. There's nothing you can do to me.

Sure, maybe. But if you let me out, I will go home and I'll delete it, and you'll never have to see me again. I pinky promise.

He's laughing again, but at what I don't know.

You dumb bitch, he says.

Everything disappears and then suddenly I'm back again. We are in front of a door in a white hallway—my door. Fuck, I'm such an idiot.

Open it, he says. My keypad is flashing red.

Why should I? I ask.

Because if you don't, I'm going to hang out around here until someone comes, and I'm going to wait until they go inside, follow behind them and slit their throat.

I think about Ivy skipping up here and feel panic shudder through me as I imagine him following behind her, and then—I can't handle thinking about it. I make decisions that sometimes put me in harm's way and I think I'm better than most at bearing the results, but only when it's me taking the punishment.

Okay fine, you win. I say the code.

The keypad makes that happy ding sound and he turns the lock, and I've never hated a robot more in my life.

As we walk through the kitchen, the dahlias sitting on the countertop look more like imploding stars than they did before with their aging droop. He throws open the door to my bedroom violently, and it ricochets off the living room wall.

Where is your phone? he demands.

It's in the beside table.

He pulls it open and grabs my phone.

Code?

Same as the door.

He puts it in and struggles to find the photos app, before he begins to tap through the photos, one by one.

This will take years, can't I just do it?

He pauses for a moment, and says Fine. But try anything and I swear I will kill your friend when they come.

I understand.

For the second time since that brief moment the night before, I find myself in control of his hands. He is too distracted focusing on the pictures that I'm deftly navigate with his left hand to notice his right drifting back toward the bedside table. I wait until the hand is almost in the drawer before I make my move.

With every bit of strength and willpower that I have left, I grab the honeyed handle of my switchblade and flip it upright as I swing it directly for his throat.

As the blade plunges into his Adam's apple I feel a slight pull of resistance, but it is too little and too late. My phone clatters to the ground as he falls back on the bed, arms desperately flailing at his throat to stem the cascade of blood. The pain is sharp, but worse is the gurgle of drowning when no direction could possibly bring air. Then, like a tide going out, it all begins to recede as vision blurs and limbs slump. Then, the world vanishes.

It's dark again and I am still enmeshed in flesh, but this time things are different. There is no sound of pumping blood or all of the other little things that a body does. Now, I am truly trapped in meat and meat alone.

It strikes me all at once that it's been days since I have eaten, or drank water, or anything else that keeps a person living. An all-ravenous hunger overtakes me and I suddenly feel more beast than human, and without thinking about it for a second I open my mouth wide and push my mouth onto whatever is before me, biting down hard. It slides into my mouth, sticky and wet, but I chew vigorously and swallow.

Then again, and again, and again.

I start thinking about The Very Hungry Caterpillar, a book both my parents would read to me night after night. It was the funniest thing I could imagine that he eats all these fruits, these very tasty looking fruits, but then he's still hungry even after so many and so he eats basically all the things at once. And I remember how delicious all of those foods looked—like the cherry pie, and the chocolate cake. And the pickle! I had forgotten about that, or at least not really thought about it, until now. Because I think I really now get what he meant when he said that he was hungry.

I don't know how long it has been, but I haven't stopped eating. The skin of his belly has started to collapse down onto me as I've consumed him, a thin rubber blanket conforming to my shape. I can see now from my own eyes, filtered light through the neon red of his flesh like the twilight of some alien sunset.

The skin of his belly stretches outwards and grows taught before it breaks: a satisfying ripping, noiseless, as my grasping hands and feet emerge, pushing up his white t-shirt caked in browning blood.

Pushing myself through the gnawed remains of his pried apart ribcage, I sit up. My eyes take time to adjust to the light, and through the blur it becomes clear that I'm still here, on my bed in my apartment, with Appa still staring watchfully but a bit redder than I remember. The money is gone, but I don't seem to care. A convulsive shiver runs down my spine and I cross my arms across my chest and squeeze. Looking down, I see a flabby layer of fleshy slime coating me, but I also see me: my breasts, my arms, my thighs. I move my hair, and although it feels sticky and wet I smile as it brushes my back. I wiggle my toes and feel a stray bit of Daddy fall off.

Everything is the same, but yet everything is new. I feel tears well up in my eyes as I raise up from the sack of flesh and bone below me, my knees quivering. Then, surprising even myself, with my own voice I begin to sing.

To the Shadow that Watches
Me Sleep, Breathes on My Neck, Lives
in the Corner of My Eye

by T.m. Lawson

Tonight everyone forgot me:

my nightshade teeth was a story

brothers told themselves

at 24-hour diners, guilty

of loving.

I smoke indigo,

shaping a creature

who stares

at the back of my head

when I try to sleep.

Your constant underhiss,

eyes pressed into my ear

pressing

for a break, a single

fracture

as I clutch onto any warm body

for protection against

this cool vapor

staring at me

in the dark.

If I fed you

silence, we would both

be gluttons.

If I fed you

fire, only I would get burned.

2.

I read

(somewhere) to keep secrets

grind sage to your teeth.

It tastes like spirits

who knew my name.

3.

Next to a warm pile of human,

freshly fucked,

I want to think I'm touching

the face of God. It was

you, once.

Still you whisper the virtues

of nightshade

of fruitless trees,

of being a snake

in a keyless garden, forgotten

locks complete. I admire your floral

tongue. Liars

could make songs.

If they tasted you,

they would fear you.

The Honey Locust Tree

by Leanna Moxley

Soft leaves draped over clusters of long, brown seedpods. Thick spikes sprouted right from the trunk, some as long as my arm. I slipped my hand between these thorns and touched the bark.

"What is this," my friend Bird breathed, pulling loose a seedpod. She cracked it open; inside was a thick yellow paste, sweet-smelling.

We knew all the mountain trees in the woods between her trailer and my house — pines, oaks, hickory, maple, sourwoods. This tree was fiercer in its ancient stillness. I found a patch of bark without thorns and lay my face against it, pressing my ear hard enough for pain. Warmth surged through the wood and set my body tingling. I could almost make out a voice, speaking to me, saying my name.

"Hello," I whispered.

Bird tugged my arm, "you'll get spiked."

I wanted to tell her what I was listening for, what the tree was saying, but I couldn't grasp the words, and the images grew strange and large and left my head. I pulled away and rubbed my hands on my jeans, laughing a little to break the tension.

***

Last night I dreamed I stood before the tree and it was glowing with inner light. I longed for it, hips tingling, an ache between my legs. I pulled loose one of the seedpods and split it open, brought it to my face and ran my tongue down the crease. The soft insides were sweet and slick, so delicious I shivered.

When I woke in the grey dawn my whole body was pulsing. I pulled a sweater over my nightgown, then crept downstairs so as not to wake dad, grabbed my boots, and headed for the woods.

The path led me straight to the tree. I rested my palms gently against thorns, pushing experimentally, but it wasn't pain I longed for. I needed to be closer. So I tore off thorns until I cleared a space to press my body against the trunk. Better, but not close enough. I took my clothes off, shivering in the morning air, and pressed my bare skin against the trunk. Still, not enough.

I flushed with a heat like anger, dug my fingers under the bark, and pulled. It was looser than I expected; great sheets fell to the ground. Musk rose like smoke. I went on tearing, splinters under my nails, a rush of need crawling up my throat and burning my eyes. There were deep grooves in the exposed wood, like something had been carved under the bark. I pushed my fingers into those grooves, sticky with sap, and felt warmth, pulsing, longing—something was here, if I could get it loose. I scrabbled harder until something released —the sudden lightness knocked me off balance and I fell to the ground.

I breathed heavily, staring at the tree. Sticks jabbed into my bare legs; I was naked and should feel ashamed. Rustlings rose in the brush around me. Warblers chittered overhead. Too bright for spookiness. There was a shape in the wood. The smooth outline of a body, one arm dangling loose, fingers splayed.

I dusted off, then went back to the tree and slipped my hand through the fingers. They tightened. My chest jolted. I moved my nails along the grooves again, tugging, anxious now. A crack— I pulled — something gave way — I pulled, fell, the body on top of me. I gasped for air, pushed it off, then stood up slowly.

The tree person shifted in the leaf-filtered light.

Skin polished to a warm shine.

Lids and lips parted.

Eyes like the liquid surface of a river.

"Hello," I said, like I'd said to the tree before, when it was only a tree.

Lips closed. Opened. "Hello" —a croak from deep inside.

I took the wooden fingers, now pliable as flesh. The tree

person tugged against me and pulled up to standing. We were the same height, eye to eye, nose to nose. They wrapped their arms around me. It was natural, a relief. We turned toward each other, eyes meeting. They put their mouth on mine. My hot breath and their warm wood breeze, the body pliant: my blood ran even quicker.

We came apart. "Please take me home," they said, voice small and exhausted.

"Where is home?" I asked, still spinning.

They touched my shoulder. "I need to rest."

I searched my mind for understanding but came up dry. "What should I call you?"

They seemed more naked than before; the outlines shaded in now, their body complex and alive. They squinted up at the patches of blue visible through the pines. "It's warm," they said, and it was, a soft, thick kind of warmth. "What month is it?"

"It's June."

"The time isn't right. I shouldn't be out yet. But here I am. So you can call me June."

I searched their face, but couldn't read their wooden eyes. "I'm sorry," I said, "Maybe it's my fault. I tore the bark off and pulled you out. Maybe I shouldn't have."

June frowned and traced their fingers over the space in the tree where their body had been. "You couldn't have done this if I wasn't already separating. But I can't remember. I can't hear properly. I need some time to think."

***

Out of the woods, under the garland of bees, up the hill and in the back door. It was late afternoon, so I knew my dad would be sitting on the front porch like always, watching the sky change.

In my bedroom, June gazed out the window past the hives spilling bees into the summer sky. I gazed at June's back. All their limbs were smooth and well muscled and seemed to be lit from within.

"I would like to rest a while," they said.

It was still so early in the morning. I thought of Bird, on the other side of the woods, sound asleep in her trailer. What would she think if she saw me now? Maybe, eventually, I would find a way to tell her.

I pulled back the quilt on my bed and patted the mattress. "You can rest here."

June crawled in, turned on their side, and curled up like a child. Afternoon sun fell over them, golden. I crept closer, socks hushing over the smooth, wood floor.

"Come here," June said.

I climbed in behind them. They didn't move. I fitted my body along theirs, tucking my knees into theirs, wrapping my arms around their stomach. They softened and settled. I softened, too. Our breaths came together: rise and fall, rise and fall. It wasn't long before I also sank into a wide and weighty sleep. It was the first time I'd slept so well in months.

The Vampire's Lament

by Michael Calkins

"Of course, I bit you. What did you think was going to happen? Satan's bifurcated cock! I told you what I am. Feeding on and corrupting the living is what I do. I don't want to be your boyfriend or your sugar daddy. I'm not some slicked-haired, business-suited douchebag that you can domesticate. I am a creature of metaphysical evil. And I didn't pay for dinner so I could get into your pants. I don't give a shit about what's in there.

"I'm dead. I'm room temperature. You must have felt that. My heart doesn't beat. There's no blood to flow. No blood pressure, no erection, no arousal. All I want to do is drink the blood from your body. Hell's hairy asshole! If I wasn't so hungry I'd just snap your neck right now.

"I miss the days when people knew there was such a thing as evil. When they took it seriously and were afraid. How sweet to get past their prudent caution and faith-powered crosses to drain the life from their veins. The women back then were delicious. They were redolent of frustrated desire and the fear of damnation. You stink of birth control and misapprehended capitalism. Your vague spirituality couldn't cause that cross around your neck to give me the tiniest blister.

"I should get out of this country. Go somewhere less modern and cynical. Get away from the half-believers who think it would be so cool to meet or date or be a vampire. I should go where they still know that there are dangers beyond the mundane. Of course, it would be more dangerous for me. But the thrill of it! The carefully planned hunt. The hard-earned kill. Beelzebub's festering prostate! There's the arousal. That's what makes it worthwhile. Not sucking the blood from narcissists too busy preening for their next selfie to be afraid for their lives and souls.

"Fine, let's get back to sucking your disappointing blood. It tastes of B vitamin supplements and dishonest concern for the poor. Struggle a little more, I'm about to end your life. A scream, yes. Finally, some real fear. Keep it up, just like that. A little music with my meal."

Parliament of Babies (episode one)

by Jason Squamata

I wasn't there.

But from what Violet told me and what I have dreamed and seen since knowing her, I can imagine it carefully (but completely) and I think it was something like this…

Violet, just ten then, small and pale in the restless shadows of her suburban bedroom, trembling in the frilly cage they made for her, their little darling, cluttered with all the objects a healthy girl of her time and space might like. As if they didn't even know her. Trembling from a breeze through the open window and from missing him, from missing her big brother so much that she's sick with it. It would be his birthday in just a few minutes, and he wasn't home, and the tendril-tips of her nervous system were almost stabbing through her skin from within, from her abject hunger and thirst for him. Her brother Johnny. The only one who knows her, or who knew her then.

Her walls and ceiling were plastered with glow in the dark stars and her nursery cosmos felt vast that night, she just a ghost girl or a little moon, floating in it. All that queasy light. All that bubbling darkness. And the real stars, churning through the blurry lens of her fever, through a scrim of lacy gauze, through the pretty wound of a window. She trembled for several forevers, wondering if his great change would come to pass, if he could unfold fully without her watching and doing the movements. There's nothing for her to pray to but the beast on the other side of his shifting. But prayers can sometimes summon things, even if you don't know what shade of angel might be listening and pulling some strings.

And then there he was, the brother, climbing in through her window in soggy hospital clothes, pungent bughouse pyjamas, a twelve year old refugee from the land of Nod, going on thirteen and never coming back. But in the little bedroom with her, suddenly summoned, suddenly real, so much more actual than the dolls and the painted rainbows and the cartoon taxidermy.

Sprawled in a Disney-skinned puddle of tree-scarred moonlight. As pale as she, with Peter Pan freckles and eyes too tired for a face so young, but lighting up at the sight of her, at the smile she'd break into whenever he made mischief.

They must have kissed like symbiotic siblings kiss. They must have held each other.

He was soaked with something and he smelled like the scary garage, but she didn't care. What trials must he have endured to survive and escape that place on this special night? She couldn't imagine. It was her nature to forgive him everything always and sacramentalise his every defect.

They must have savoured the reunion and communion with a special intensity. Considering what they'd been through, what they knew. Knowing the hell that must come to him in this room in a matter of moments, otherwise a story is just a story and the things they said aren't true. Johnny was as hungry for Violet's proximity as she had been for his. But the process they serve is higher than love. A transcendental process, though they didn't use those words.

Johnny was a religion unto himself. Violet was his only apostle.

Three years between them, but he deferred to her always, with a sincere reverence, since way back, since before his hysterical revelations and their religious conversations and the strange secret games they played that changed everything. In Johnny's mind, Violet was closer to the thing they were before the beginning of things, and therefore more holy than he. But he was so close to tasting that place and state again. It's what birthdays are all about.

She would follow him into any old nightmare. His way of seeing made sense of everything in ways the tired monotone myths of the grown-ups did not.

He asked her if she remembered what to do. Because of this desperate improvisation, they couldn't employ all the elements of this ritual they had rehearsed so often they could do it in dreams. But so much of it was window dressing anyway, all the props and the incantations. It really all comes down to acoustics and chemistry.

Of course she remembered.

The kitchen matches she stole for him were hidden in the dollhouse. They did foresee some emergencies. She handed him the box and hated the hurting but loved him and believed him, and there is no death, if you know the ritual tones and poses. Only a change of state. No words were necessary. No noise but a tone only children can hear. No haggard parent would wake up to stop this, not until it was too late.

He sat Indian style at the foot of her ridiculous princess bed, opening the matchbox, sharing a brave gaze with her. She sat on the bed and contorted into a configuration of limbs only a child could achieve. She was a Möbius strip of girlflesh, wearing a doll mask, staring through him and into him with the innocence of a mirror.

At the very same moment, they emitted the tone. A vibrational lubricant that smooths the birthing of something Other as it sloughs its little kid cocoon. It's what we're here for. It's the big secret. The big secret I know now because she told me. Striking a match. Still, the tone. A complicated grace attended their ceremony. The first strike made flame.

Flame unfolding like the wavering petals of a solarized timelapse ghost lily, licking his surface with pyjama-shredding, skin-blistering heat. Just like in his visions. Still, they made the tone. Despite the flame. Despite the pain. Louder now, just a minute or two until the adulty things come shambling through the door, stinking like they do of decay and shrivelled convictions.

Still, the gaze and the tone, and already he was beyond pain, his babyskin blackened into ash and brainjuice boiling, consciousness in ruins. Still, the lotus, like a young monk in wartime. The whole bedroom catching fire, then. His heart burst and something inside him was ready to leave and her gaze didn't waver.

Her dollhouse was a hot pink holocaust. The dolls themselves were burning as they beheld him, as they bore witness to a metamorphosis perceptible only to mad children and their playthings. Johnny's lungs were dust, but Violet went right on chanting until the parentals came running in, all electric with anxiety like always. As electric as they get.

The happening that kept Violet still despite the heat and the horror of it all and serene despite her violently disintegrating playmate, that event was invisible to the eye of "maturity". All the parents saw that night was their allegedly incarcerated thirteen-year old son on fire in his little sister's bedroom, wayward boy smoked into charcoal bones. Their daughters limbs twisted in some kind of acrobatic evil tween yoga, emitting a ghostly tone that afflicted them with phantom aches in every tooth they had lost since they were children.

The male parent screamed. The female lunged and seized her daughter, screaming too but fast and brave like a child, just for a moment. A moment was enough to save suddenly silent Violet, who let it happen.

She'd seen the shifting.

She knew it to be true then, in her nerves instead of just in her head, all the mad things Johnny had known and shared with her since before they started wrapping her up in words. She had emitted the tone, she had watched it all, and she didn't cry. Her mask was incorruptible, for it framed the flames in her own future. There's a place that is not a place where the thing we really are pleasures itself with many tendrils that dream that they are individuals until they are flexed and we remember. She would breathe him there, in the fullness of time. She had some growing to do. Rules. Always rules. No state has more rules than freedom.

Outside and "safe", more alone with the old ones than ever, and yet full of Johnny and his triumph, she savoured the chaos. She liked the sirens and the flashing lights and the way their burning house lit up the screaming sky and the abyss itself was solarised, a broken girl with soft black stars in her eyes. The woman thing was holding her and turning to shield Violet's gaze from the inferno where her sick brother died before her eyes. But Violet was squirming and determined to see it all, apocalypse and aftermath, and commit every hungry tongue of flame to memory.

She rebuffed the shrill consolations of the man and the woman and all the other misshapen grown things on the street in their nightclothes. She could see hints in the incendiary afterbirth of her brother's transfiguration that made her laugh out loud.

Laughing madly, like every little thing in the burning world was funny. Laughing like that for too many minutes.

When the old doctor things gave her something druggy and the laughing stopped, Violet dreamed of a haunted world without him, only three years long. How should she spend those breathless hours? How could she honor him in that time and make his achievement understood? By other kids, that is. No one else matters. Not even the parentals. Especially not the parentals. They'll run from brutal truth, like grown-ups do. They'll take her away from all this, as if to start anew.

New places.

New friends.

New games.

"Games tend to end," he would say, "but a lot goes on forever."

"INCUBATORIUM"
by Jason Squamata

in your shadow gallery

where the forms escape their frames,

formulas flow, feed, and breed

and play their wicked games.

in your cellular library

where the numbers on the spines

indicate taste, shape, and fate

your index will be mine.

i'm born again

every now and then

where my invisible friends

await a game of let's pretend.

you struck me dumb

but where would i run?

when the world is just a womb

in your incubatorium.

in your dew-slick spiderweb

where your acolytes recline

in a blissful trance, the dust-motes dance

and fall outside of time.

in your coral abattoir

your meat meets mine at last.

my soul is sliced by the hungry eyes

of a mermaid made of glass.

i'm born again

every now and then

where my invisible friends

await a game of let's pretend.

you struck me dumb

but where would i run?

when the world is just a womb

in your incubatorium.

i've gone beyond the fields i know.

where did all the lifeforms go?

they're vanishing like footprints in the snow.

around the bend, between the scenes,

there's a city where you weave my dreams.

receive me in your ruins, sweet machine.

in your incubatorium

where geometry comes to life

you engineer delirium

with red thread and a jewelled knife.

in your blue aquarium

where the sequined equations swim,

your crystal tears, blood, sweat, and cum

will marinate my sins.

i'm born again

every now and then

where my invisible friends

await a game of let's pretend.

you struck me dumb

but where would i run?

when the world is just a womb

in your incubatorium.

the world is a womb in your incubatorium

the world is a womb in your incubatorium

the world is a womb in your incubatorium

Ghost Bustin'

by Piers Rippey

CREAK
YES
A B C
NO
YES
YES

The Bedside Book of Narrow Escapes

by Glen Armstrong

We left town just before the riots.

The TV eyes, big and red

    but discreetly placed,

    caught it all:

    Tear gas and faulty fasteners.

In that little village of longer

    shadows and taller trees,

      we hid.

We disguised ourselves

    as Madame Hydra

    and Ego the Living Planet.

I had two pairs of pants

and a beach towel to wrap

around myself

on laundry day.

We tried the local cuisine.

We worked in a factory

carving sound effects,

[KA-BLAMMO] for example,

out of the foam from abandoned

couch cushions.

The overlords were happy

with our work,

and the soda jerk

resented that.

It was a simple life for a while.

When we left, we never left

a forwarding address.

The Hunter

by Mickey Collins

A new job, a new journal. If found please bring this journal to the police, for it means I have been killed by less than normal means.

Through my sources, I heard there were some missing people in a small town. People no one would care about in a dead-end town no one pays any attention to. No one except for people like me. That's how monsters get away with things; they hunt where no one thinks anyone would pay attention. I pay attention.

The town is smaller than I'd thought, but big enough to hide any number of foul creatures here.

I must be careful who I say what to. Word gets around quickly when someone sticks out. I need a drink.

That's where I saw her, dancing, singing in the bar for a couple of locals. We made eye contact. My scars itched. I'd been taken in by girls before, both normal and not. The normal ones were always crazier, at least with monsters you know what they want from you.

While she sang, I tried making nice with the bar flies. All I got were glazed-over looks. Even the bartender was clammed up.

I drank to pass the time until she finished singing. She came up to me afterwards, I have that power. I always attract danger, and women.

I guess I stared a little longer than I meant to, on account of the drink. "Can I help you?" she asked. She noticed my looks.

"I just wanted to tell you, you sounded really good." I smiled at her.

"Thank you. The name's Layla, by the way." Her voice was

singsong even off the stage. She offered her hand and I noticed a lack of claws. A good start.

I introduced myself and offered to get her a drink. She accepted, of course.

We talked for a bit. She wasn't much of a talker, which in my experience meant she only wanted one thing. I asked her back to my hotel room.

I'm a great judge of character. Scars aside, I've been at this occupation a long time and haven't been killed yet.

I'm a little surprised to find her in my bed this morning as I write up last night's events. The hangover isn't a surprise and makes it a little hard to remember everything. But I do feel happy. Something I haven't been feeling in a long time on the road. My head itches a bit. Mosquito probably got in last night and feasted on me. Damn parasites. She's waking up now.

I offered her breakfast, but she said she had to go. I wasn't feeling hungry either, I admitted. But she couldn't even stay for coffee. I supposed I had better follow up on some leads, try and find the missing persons' next of kins. No luck. They were all loners.

As I sit in this diner, I can't stop smiling as I think of her. Even while I went around asking questions of the townsfolk, I had to stifle myself. My mind isn't on food or the missing guys anymore. It's just her.

I should go back to the bar. It isn't just a coincidence that most of the folk had been drunks, hung out at the bar most of the time. But maybe I'd see her again. I sure hoped so.

Signs seem to point to the bartender. Quiet, serving up drinks. Wondering if he maybe spiked my drink, why I'm feeling so good, why I'm wanting to go back… Or is it the girl?

The bartender still didn't say much when I started to pry. Just that some regulars haven't been seen in weeks. No real problem, except for their drink tabs. If it weren't for me trying to stay incognito, I'd think about taking him outside and getting him to talk. She'd be impressed. But I can't draw any attention. She's up on stage singing again. Instead I offer to pay off the drunks' tabs. That lightens his mood, and my wallet considerably.

"Did you notice anyone unusual hanging around them before they left?"

"No, not really."

"Did they know each other?"

"Outside of the bar? No, I don't think so."

"Any weird behavior?"

"Apart from their normal drunk rants, one of them started acting especially crazy the day I last saw him. He was convinced that I was poisoning him. I let him go for a while, he wasn't hurting anyone, but then he started going after Layla. Said she was the enemy or something. I kicked him out after that and I haven't seen him since. That was maybe two weeks ago. He was a regular before that, but I'm not offended if he found another sucker to listen to his problems. Especially with how he left."

Layla was finished with her set, as I finished up with the bartender. There was something about her, something my gut was telling me to look closer into.

"Last night was fun." Or maybe it was just my dumb old heart pulling me toward her.

"Yeah, you seemed to have a good time," she cooed back at me.

"Did you want to do it again sometime? Maybe, oh I don't know, 20 minutes?" I needed to have her again. It was a thirst I couldn't control.

She laughed. "You come on strong, don't you?"

"You should know." I laughed.

She seemed reserved, then suddenly she reversed. "Ya know

what, why not?”

It actually took me by surprise. I had a string of questions for her as we walked back to my hotel, but she danced around all of them like she did on stage.

Sorry I haven’t written in a while. Layla and I have been seeing more and more of each other. Except tonight. She said she had something else to do, but that was fine by me. It’s supposed to be a full moon tonight, a time when the supernatural is more active, so I wouldn’t want her to be out anyways, even if she was protected by me I wouldn’t want to be responsible for another one.

I decided to take the night off, from Layla, and focus back on the case, if there even is a case. Since I’ve been in town, there haven’t been any more attacks reported. Perhaps the creature took one look at me and fled for the next town. I wouldn’t blame him.

I patrol the town anyways. It’s awfully quiet and awfully dark, pitch black except for the moonlight in some places. I keep looking over my shoulder. I naturally find my way to the bar, even though Layla isn’t performing tonight, I promised her I would stay away, so I keep walking by.

I can’t keep my promise to leave her alone like she asked. Especially when it’s a full moon night. The shadows seem alive tonight. I call her, but she doesn’t pick up. I would go over to her place if I knew where she lived, but we always ended up in my hotel room. I tried calling a few more times. I’ve left a couple of messages, and a dozen texts. I need to see her.

I was finally able to get ahold of her. She told me she had a friend in town last night, which is why she wanted her privacy. Who is this friend? More important than me?

I love her.

She keeps giving me the brush off. Brushing me off? I'm tired. Feeling tired more and more. It must be this sleepy little town. Nothing's been going on for weeks. But there's something here. I know it. I should move on but I can't. I asked Layla to leave with me. She says she can't.

Another Layla-less night. I'm at the bar despite her...her... whatever. She's not here.

In the alleyway next to the bar I heard a trash can get knocked over. In the dark I could see a drunkard, no two drunkards, stumbling. I decided not to get involved and continue down the road.

And then I heard a scream. And Layla's voice? By the time I was back in the alley, the drunks were gone. I couldn't shake the feeling I heard Layla in the alley, but maybe I heard her voice coming from inside the bar?

Layla's banging on the door. My hotel door. I saw her in the alley with another man, but she was attacking him. Through the door she's saying it was self-defense. That he was getting handsy with her after her performance.

But I was in the bar. She wasn't there. He was screaming. Why was he screaming?

She's a monster. Why didn't I see this coming? The paranoia, psychotic episodes, the headaches. I always fall for them.

If this is my last journal entry, then so be it. At least I'll go out swinging.

The Monster

by Hannah Broadbent

By day I spend my time like any regular human would. I have a dead-end job (that makes me feel so normal), a small apartment and I might be able to adopt a cat if I can manage not to... anyway, by night I sing at a local bar. It's such a rush. Nowhere near the rush of feeding but it helps. I've tried everything: cows, horses, sheep. Nothing works. Nothing is as good as people taste. I have to admit, I go to this little rinky-dink bar to feed. I don't do it a lot, just enough. I figure no one is going to miss the men that spend hours there.

There's one guy that came in. He was different. Different than the old lowlifes that came in. I had never seen him before. He looked...nice. That night, after I was walking off the stage, he approached me. It startled me at first but I had to quickly remind myself to act human. I turned around quickly, "Can I help you?" That had sounded nicer in my head. "I just wanted to tell you, you sounded really good." He smiled at me. "Thank you, my name's Layla by the way." I stuck out my hand like any normal human would. "Hey, I'm David, nice to meet you. Wanna grab a drink?" He smelled so nice. A mix of pine and a certain scent I just can't put my finger on. My stomach growled. "A drink sounds great."

We talked for hours. Or rather he talked and I listened. I try not to talk too much about my personal life. What would I even say? 'Hi, I'm Layla and I suck brain fluid out of humans. Nice to meet you, potential dinner!' Yeah, real romantic. David told me what he was doing in such a small town. He said he was on a job. It sounded like he couldn't say much so I didn't push. However, that did make me suspicious. I've heard from other... creatures, that there are hunters that have been making their way through the country offing monsters. That's the last thing I need, some burly dude coming through and killing me while I'm trying to live a normal life. In the meantime, I was going to enjoy the life I chose with this handsome stranger.

David asked if I wanted to go back to his hotel room. I had never done such a thing but I figured that's what people do, so let's try it. We arrived and well, I won't go into details but I had never experienced anything like it before. Feeding is one thing, but sex is a whole new ball game. Afterwards, he fell asleep and I couldn't help myself. He just smelled so good and looked so beautiful, I had an itch that needed to be scratched. I didn't take much, just enough to get a taste. Nothing to damage him to the point of no return. It felt so good. I felt *whole* again. After my midnight snack I fell asleep alongside him.

The next morning he woke up before me. I had overslept. I wanted to get out before he had woken. I don't want to make a habit out of sleeping with humans but I suppose it's a part of their lifestyle. He tried getting me to eat some stale doughnuts and coffee he got at the diner down the street. The smell alone made me gag. I ran out of his room almost as fast as it took for me to get into his pants. Once I got back home I hoped I wouldn't run into him again. I started remembering some scars he had on his chest. Most human males don't have *that* many scars, right? I started becoming more paranoid as the day went on. I decided to slow down on my feeding until I knew David was out of town. That night I went back to the bar to perform again, hoping to get that rush once more. As I opened the door I saw him talking to the bartender, Bill. David saw me and flashed a quick smile. I just nodded at him and went to the stage to set up. *Do I talk to him? Is it more suspicious if I don't?* I was trying to hear what he was asking Bill about but it was hard to hear over the music playing from the jukebox. It looked like he was questioning Bill, which wasn't a good sign.

After my set was done I started packing up my things. David came over to me. "Last night was fun." Such a romantic. "Uh, yeah. You seemed to have a good time," I chuckled. "Well, you wanna do that again sometime? Maybe, oh I don't know, 20 minutes?" I scoffed and replied, "Wow you come on strong, don't you?" "You should know." He laughed as I rolled my eyes. My stomach flipped when I caught a whiff of his piney scent. "Ya know what, why not?" His eyes were about to pop out of that juicy head of his.

So, once again I went to his hotel room and we had an incredible time. As I laid there, staring at his chest rising and falling, I couldn't help but trace my fingers over his scars. My heart pounded out of excitement, or maybe it was nervousness. *Is this what love feels like?* I wanted to just lay there for hours and watch him sleep. I got closer to him and well, I'm ashamed to say the least. I told myself I would stop but something about him, I just can't help myself. I've been so used to feeding off of those dirty old men at the bar. David is just so different. He's charming and strong. I could easily see us spending the rest of our lives together if it weren't for...me.

Nights go by and I try my best to control my urges. Some nights are better than others. Some nights he won't stop calling and others he ravages my body and I ruin any chance of us becoming more than just monster and monster's dinner. I tried going back to the bar. The lowlifes. They taste disgusting to me now. I was in the back alley behind the bar and this scruffy old man I was feeding on wouldn't shut up. I was getting loud too and I'm afraid someone might have heard us. I'm getting sloppy. What the fuck is wrong with me?

I threw my fists at David's hotel door. I know he heard me. I saw him outside the bar when I was going back inside that night. I told him the old man hurt me, that he was trying to touch me. David wasn't buying it. He said, "The man was yelling for help, why would *he* be calling for help?" He kept repeating that question over and over. I left before it got out of hand. I just had to go back, didn't I?

David said it's unnatural to love something like me. Some *thing*.

I felt a jolt of pain go through my chest, the back of my neck felt cold while my face was burning. I launched myself towards him and we fell to the floor. I took him by surprise and was able to over-power him. We tossed and turned but this time it wasn't the act of love that started it. We were struggling for awhile, me straddling his chest; I grabbed a lamp off the bedside table and hit him over the head with it. He was knocked unconscious and as his limp body laid on the hotel floor I realized that I'll never change. I'll always be a monster.

Untitled
by Andy Anderson

Seasons are changing

Temperatures dropping

The last stick of incense burns on my altar

Smoke fills the room slowly

Like a spell

But this story isn't about magic

But bodies

My body

A cave to my hibernation

Insecurity floating toward balance

My hair growing out

I am growing out

Of this body

I prepare

Count my blessings

Count my friends

Pull in the harvest of the garden

And embrace me

This body

Our appointment arrives

She changes her clothes

A red gown

She has been bitten

And so I will too

Everything happens

Yet Nothing happens

She suffocates me

Chokes me

Darkness in the night

And together we collapse

Into bed

The wood creaks

Our breath constricts

Heartbeats quicken

Reality pauses as my chest heaves

We lay in wake all night

Wounds bound

This old body and

Her fresh bloody body

One

We rest all day

In dreams

As the warmth wanes

Our preparation for the trauma was enough

The blood and the love now together

Self-love and nourishment that came with

The heat

The fruit

The symptoms

Then

Together we came

With the

Kill

Together

with the bite

The equinox arrives

And this gathering

This night, the

Marks on our necks

Yours a celebration

Mine an awakening

Our coven solidifies and

Like Mabon we wait to be reborn

Dreams discern into signs

An abundant harvest

Just like that

My chest heaves

And my eyes open

The sun has set

The smoke gone

The sheets white

The ghosts are all that's left

I thirst

Feel my neck

My bites no longer wounds

I ask

Are vampires even real?

am I even real?

The Sun and Her Shadow

by Timothy Merritt

When the stars began to wink into existence across an inky night, the earth stirred beneath a Glastonbury field and the first few inches of a finger birthed through. One finger was followed by others, pale towers rising from the underground, until a whole hand emerged straining for purchase in the soft dark soil, slowly beginning to grip and pull.

The man that emerged from the ground that night had long forgotten his name; a blank slate shaking the soil from his pale skin. He was not possessed of much identity at all, instead filled with a singular desire to search skyward, to scan among the pinpricks of distant light for the only sight that might cure his affliction. He was looking for her.

The Man From the Earth knew only that she had hidden herself in that panoply of fire in the days when the sky was still young and much smaller. In those primitive days she had gleamed as a brilliant beacon amongst paltry lesser lights, and had guided the man and others like him through the long night. Now though, there were countless stars above, and they seemed to have grown smaller and more distant over the eons. His nightly search for her light thus inevitably ended always in failure and sense of deep shame when he returned to the earth at the tail of each evening, crawling back into the dirt in that small clearing that sat in the shadow of that hard-capped hill of Glastonbury Tor, where a roofless church tower stood like an arrow towards the sky.

On this night, however, the Man From the Earth was sure of himself. He was sure —as he was each night—that this would finally be the night he would catch sight of the beloved light he missed so dearly, so inexplicably, and once found he would go to her and join her in the sky for all eternity. The Man From the Earth was perhaps blinded by the surety of his love for this nearly forgotten light, but what else is there but blind pursuit when one has lost all purpose and memory in the face of a love burned down to its aching core?

He made his usual cursory scan of the heavens, all the lights there blending into a ubiquity of faintness that bred in him the first feelings of frustration for that night. Hers was not the kind of light to be so diminished, so diminutive. No, he knew, despite the geological ages that had passed since he last felt her heat upon his face, that hers was a flame that no other could rival, and was nothing like the cool, pale sphere that sometimes grew and shrank to a sliver overhead. Hers was a fire than lit infernos in the heart of humankind.

The Man From the Earth stayed there for a few hours, neck craned at a futile angle before the strain became too much for him and he cast his gaze lower, watching the mists roll over the sleeping town of Glastonbury, and decided perhaps he would stroll the droves that linked its green places for a while to distract himself from the rising cloud of melancholy in his mind.

Though he walked aimlessly, his path took him closer to the Tor, that high hill that had stood for millennia. As he followed the grassy paths towards it, eventually beginning to snake his way up its inclines, his eyes were never far from the sky for long. There was an ache that rent through his chest with each breath, a feeling that told him with certainty that his beloved was not here, and that at the end of night he would crawl back into his pit to sleep cold and alone and wait for his next chance to seek her out again.

He had nearly run into the old church tower atop the hill before he stopped walking. Here was St. Michael's Tower, an imposing relic from centuries past made of tapering stone reaching towards the firmament. The Man From the Earth faced the open archway that led through the structure, gazing into the solid darkness within. A strange thought crept into him. Perhaps he could wait in that darkness for his beloved to come to him? Perhaps on this high hill, not buried below the earth and hidden from her view, she would more readily be able to seek him out in turn? The sudden prospect then that she had perhaps done so, parsing away the ages with the self-same mixture of dedication and hopelessness that he himself had, filled him with a renewed hope—along with a vivid sense of stupidity. But would she see him secluded in such covering? Would she find him hidden under the stone? Yes, he decided, for her light was brilliant and strong, and she could find any man no matter what cave or cowl he hid beneath.

Weary from his walk and the dimming hope that he might ever see that disarming light again, the Man From the Earth lay down in the open space within the tower's archway, reveling in the strange but not unwelcome sensation of sleeping upon soft grass, rather than beneath it. He soon fell into a deep, dreamless sleep.

What was meant to be a short spell of sleep became a long, restful slumber for the man of the earth, and when pale, pink twilight tinted the horizon he was still snoring softly upon his green bed. The sun rose heavy in the east, dispelling the clinging mists and cool, dewy air from the countryside, and the night became morning.

When the day's light reached the archway of the tower the shadows crept away in inches, until shade no longer touched any part of the man and he woke to the warm embrace of that legendary star. He blinked away sleep and tried to drink in the unfamiliar light that filled the world around him, until his senses returned to him and a sharp pang of remembrance dug deep into his heart.

The sun! That glorious fireball called Sol, and Magec, and Beiwe, and by all her other names shone down on him with an embrace of light and heat that acted like a restorative, rebirthing memories that had long been washed away into the shadowy depths of his mind. Here was his star. Here was the brilliance he had once stood inside, the heat that had fed upon his body like fire on fresh coals. He stood up in the archway to face her, to stare unblinking into her single searing eye, welcoming the flash of pain the view brought. His body was nearly translucent in its paleness after so long a time spent in her absence, and it began to blister and burn at once. The pain was excruciating, yet the Man From the Earth was unperturbed, his lips splitting as much from the fiery rays above as from the wide smile that formed where only a staunch grimace had stood for millennia. His hair caught flame, momentarily giving him the image of a grotesque candle before the rest of his body followed, and the Man From the Earth became a Man of the Sun.

In the noon-day sunshine, seemingly brighter that day then it had been in recent memory, the visitors to Glastonbury Tor that came for photos and compartmentalized grandeur were treated to a strange, unexpected sight. Within the famous archway of

St. Michael's Tower, one of the best places on the hill for souvenir photos to be taken, a two-foot wide ring of black was seared upon the ground. A small pile of ash was gathered at its center, which after tourists notified one of the grumbling groundskeepers, was brushed discreetly away into the surrounding grasses. The ring, however, remained, and each morning the sun's light would fall upon it as it rose in the east, heating the earth there in its warm embrace.

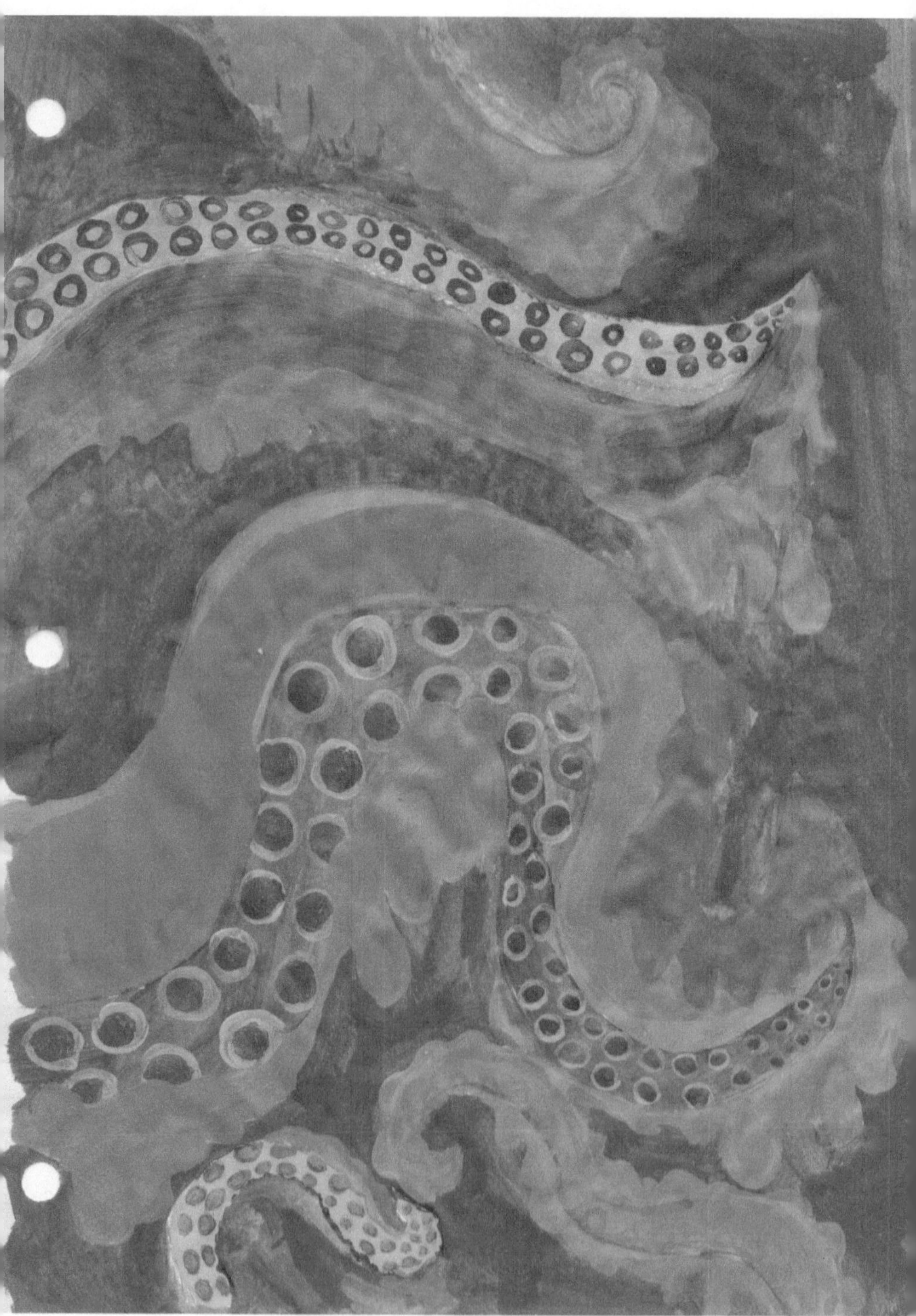

You Think Your Tendrils Clicked In—

by Maya McOmie

and I do creep into your weird

grossness. Although I reel

at the absurd, the anthropomorphic: when you

unify jagged things, I spasm. It's not

that I fear the tentacles: nor that snakes,

slinking, or the buttery gut punch

of a jellyfish hold jurisdiction.

I don't mean claws—gruesome, stark—

can clench: they cannot grasp.

Whatever I expected, it was not this.

Backwards advancement: an education

in alien code. Known voice

unfamiliar within glints of projection.

What I mean: syncopation makes

injury gleam unremarkably

acceptable. What I do not say:

this is recast. Of all of my

ruses, past-blasted, best rested.

You trace the membrane's

framework as if you

never knew circles until now.

What would it take to retire

you to apparition. If I could

reinvent the three eyes,

purplish lips: but of course

you function too well, unremorseful.

When singled out each small

exaggeration seems exhausted.

I might seek relentless, a questioning orb.

I cannot eat, blue from warning,

cannot sleep until indulged. So:

strength my unbecoming.

I know: this won't be how I

turn. My inner tone holds

an even inflection. I am

sparse: without qualifiers, calmness

in a storm's eye. I cannot bear

self within me.

A Love Hate Relationship

by Kimberly Owen

Love was a complete mystery, and Hate couldn't get enough. Perched on the edge of their heart-shaped bed, he watched with fascination as she slept. Her charcoal hair lay across her face, a strand rising and falling with each breath. Hate reached forward with a small hand, but stopped inches from Love's face. If he moved her hair, the disturbance might wake her and Love didn't like it when he woke her up. In fact, Love didn't like anything Hate did, but rather than be deterred by her attitude, it only made him more determined to please her. Humming, he walked over to the window and pushed it open, letting the morning sunshine and birdsong fill the room.

"Shut those birds up, will you?" Love grumbled, still half asleep. Turning over, she nestled deeper into the red velvet sheets.

"Ah, morning, Love. Did you sleep well?" Hate asked, as a small blue bird landed on his outstretched hand. He whistled softly and the bird responded with a musical whistle of its own. Everyone liked Hate, even the animals. Giggling, he said, "Look how cute this bird is, Love. Almost as cute as you."

Love groaned. Did he have to be so happy all the time? It didn't matter how badly she treated him, how many names she called him or how often she kicked him, he still adored her. His whole existence irritated her. Rather than respond to him, she pulled the covers over her head and ignored him.

"What shall we do today, Love?" The thick bedding muffled Hate's cheerful voice, but it still made her want to vomit. She needed to get rid of him. A hot new guy had arrived in town and Love had big plans for him.

"Anything that doesn't involve me having to look at your face," she sniped, throwing the covers on to the floor. Sitting up, she looked at him with disgust, but he didn't notice. He never did, and the more he desired her, the more she despised him.

Flicking her hair, Love walked over to the full-length mirror in the corner of their bedroom and began thinking of the things she had in store for Dream, the young man who would be keeping her company this afternoon.

Unaware of her plans to betray him, Hate admired Love's beauty and thought, not for the first time, how lucky he was to have her.

"How about I make your favourite kebabs for tea?" he asked, skipping toward her. "Although, I will have to go out of town to get some more skewers. The last one we had bent when you tried to stab me in the leg with it, remember?"

Love couldn't keep the smile off her face. Her lips parted in triumph because Hate would be away from the house all day and her eyes sparkled with nostalgia as she remembered how good trying to stab the idiot in the leg had felt. Of course, Hate misinterpreted them both.

"There we go. I knew the thought of kebabs would make you happy." He leaned forward and planted a kiss on Love's cheek, not registering her shudder of revulsion. "I'll get going right away. See you later, my Love."

Left alone, Love retrieved her mobile phone from the bedside table and sent Dream a text message. Humming to herself, she began to prepare herself for his arrival.

Less than two hours later, Hate was on his way back home. He'd been out of town to buy a brand new set of kebab skewers, but his visit to the supermarket had been cut short by Poseidon who'd flooded the entire shop because of an unexpected item in the bagging area. He didn't like letting Love down, but Poseidon's temper was well known around town and Hate knew she'd understand.

Love, otherwise engaged with her young Dream, didn't hear Hate's key turning in the lock of the front door or the sound of his footsteps as he made his way up the stairs to their bedroom. In fact, Love only became aware of his presence in the room when Dream's sweat-soaked body was lifted off her own.

"You bitch!" Hate's voice sounded nothing like his own. It was filled with a pain Love had never encountered before. She barely noticed as Dream scuttled out of the open bedroom door, grabbing his clothes as he went.

She covered herself with one of the red velvet sheets. "Hate, I'm sorry. Let me explain," she wailed, getting up to go to him. The remorse she felt confused her and the tears pouring from Hate's pale eyes hurt her in a way she didn't understand. When he turned his back on her, it broke her heart. She moved toward him on legs which weren't quite steady and her hand trembled as she raised it to his shaking shoulders. Before her hand reached him, Hate turned toward her and the look in his eyes burned right through to her soul. It was the last thing Love would ever see. A searing pain ripped through her face and the sickly copper taste of blood filled her mouth as she bit into her tongue. The world went dark and she struggled to stay on her feet. Hearing the front door slam hard enough to shake the frame, Love understood what Hate had done. Consumed with rage at catching her in bed with Dream, he'd stabbed her in the eyes with the skewers he had so lovingly purchased for her. Her screams filled the air, but there was no one there to hear them.

Now, Hate crushes the earth beneath his heavy feet and each footstep he takes leaves a crater where nothing will ever grow again. Since leaving Love behind, he no longer thinks coherently. He no longer sees the good in anything, he destroys indiscriminately and leaves nothing but pain and misery in his wake.

Love follows, always arriving too late. All she wants is to repair the misery she caused and heal Hate's broken heart. She tries to make amends for the destruction he causes, but being blind she often makes things worse instead.

They are now destined to travel the Earth, always out of each other's reach because Love and Hate cannot reside together in the same place.

The Moon and the Wolf

by Ben Talley

There has never been a connection so strong as was the bond between the Moon and the Wolf.

The Wolf, by day a man bored and lifeless, became his true self at night within the glow of its love. There were many days when he could feel its lingering presence in the bright light sky above, keeping him company through the drudgery of his average existence. Each day it would beckon him, hover about his mind and over his head, a constant reminder of joys that awaited him when the sun fell. And when it did, he felt free like no other. At the hour that the moon's glow, faint or righteous, beamed from its starstudded throne the man would be ripped from his human-born shell and rebirthed. Amidst spilt blood and broken bone he was reborn. Fur and fang, paw and claw, this was what the Moon made him. This was what it wanted, what it desired. Not the man that the world had chosen him to be, but the beast. Stagnation was traded for passion, a mumble for a howl.

It was in this embrace that he became what he always knew he could be. This was the way the moon wanted him, and he couldn't be more proud to please. He would gladly race through the forests and shout his love into the open sky each night for it. The moon's influence was undeniable. He only wished for more.

For how many nights can lover influence lover from across a room before one must bridge the distance? The Wolf could feel the Moon's push and pull, the cold, pleasant embrace of its light, but never its touch. These desires that burned in his mind as he hunted only grew hotter when he realized how lonely the Moon must feel. It gives him so much from so far away, yet all he can do is announce his appreciation for its gifts. It was unaccept-able, this onesided love.

During the long days while the Wolf and Moon rested the man was hard at work. The junkyard he ran had never served a purpose so resolute before. What was once a defining factor in the meaninglessness of his life quickly became the means to an end. He worked tirelessly, ripping apart the cars and appliances that littered his property and piecing them together carefully, strategically, all the while holding in mind an image of freedom. The one thing that could unite the beast inside with the faraway Moon.

He finished building the rocket an hour before dusk. He tightened the last bolt, polished the last panel, and went about saying goodbye to the man he was. Sunlight had already begun to filter from the sky and with that came the brightening of the Moon, and the changes beneath his skin. Hair began to sprout from bare skin as he turned out the lights and locked the door to his office and his home. By the time he climbed into the rocket his ankles and snout had already begun to stretch. By liftoff he was man no more.

The Wolf took flight.

His bones rattled with the ship's hull as they broke the sound barrier, but fear never shook him. He closed his eyes going up, up, up, and recalled the night of his first transformation. The cold, the dark, the screams. It was glorious. A welcome and familiar memory in that instant. And, much like that night, the intensity that seemed to stretch for a fleeting eternity came to a sudden end. The rocket had broken through the atmosphere. Silence followed.

Peace.

Night surrounded him.

He was held captive by the stars' warm embrace. Time passed without rush. Dawn would never come for him again; never force him back to the daytime flesh.

The Moon came upon him quickly.

The Wolf braced for impact. Storms of moon dust dispersed into thin air as rocket met ground. A trail was carved out by the nose and the hull in a slowing halt. Once settled, the Wolf opened the hatch and was greeted by grey snowfall. Many a winter had prepared him for the chill, and he found comfort in the familiar welcome. The moment passed and the air became clear, and with it the horizon. His love stretched for as far as his eyes could see. It was beautiful.

He dropped, curling his neck into the soft ground and kicking up dirt with his paws. Dust sifted through his fur and coated his mane. He tumbled and moaned like a pup in snow. He wanted to bury himself in the Moon's bosom.

Finally, burrowed deep into the cold refreshing ground, he felt comfort. The Moon held the Wolf; the Wolf nuzzled the Moon; neither of them alone any longer in the night.

END

Year of the Sea Monkey VIII
by Glen Armstrong

We sink into the water.

It's the closest thing to making

love in outer space,

which in turn, I understand,

is the closest thing

to one of the ancient gods

chuckling at the divine

and ancient equivalence

of a firefly.

We join the jellyfish

club, and six to eight weeks later,

Aquaman arrives at our doorstep

with our certificate.

We value our privacy,

though I get why it strikes some people

odd to hear me say that.

I'm only telling you this

because we're such good friends

and there's an off chance

that you can help me figure out

if we're the chuckle or the fly.

The Parable of the Three-Legged Stool

by L. Fid

one

There I was, fat, dumb and happy. A three-legged stool.

A glint on the horizon demanded my attention, then it was gone.

My leg. Gone! The southwestern one.

Involuntarily, I reeled back, northeast. I wobbled slightly, then somehow achieved a precarious balance on my remaining two legs.

I surveyed the situation, as best I could in my panic, without moving the slightest. I saw nothing -- nothing else, besides, well, you know -- out of the ordinary. No glints, no kindling debris, no smoking ozone burn.

Naturally, I mostly feared an unseen wind, or a sudden change of any sort, might knock me over. I was staying upright, but what of the internal mechanism maintaining this balance? Could it slow, unwind, turn off?

I tried to identify the processes ongoing in my remaining components but could not visualize the magic widget.

I then wondered if it was some aspect of my consciousness. I wandered down this path, trying to identify an archetypal psychological strand, to run experiments, and then to control it -- this part of my mind. That's what I needed to do. This was what I was thinking about, anyway, when it came on.

I started wobbling again, badly. I fought, wildly and to worse effect.

Finally, I fell. I just gave in, accepted the inevitble.

But then my body, broken and disfigured, limbless and off-balance, caught me and steered me upright again. My body, this two-legged stool.

Well, a stool no more. I am not to be sat upon.

two

I am bored, thought the two-legged stool.

She had meditated, somewhat as before, somehow managing to hold a center within the mind-racing vortex of distress and worry over her life-altering disfigurment. She emerged through that vortex, high above a desolate plain where god-driven herds mass, before realizing she had been asleep and waking up, to this.

Feeling suddenly queasy, as if she might keel over forward, she willed herself to lean back. At the expense of a few frightful wobbles, she learned to will herself forwards and back, around a small arc -- her seat askew from high to low.

She must have an adjastable center of balance, the best she could tell.

But she was not going to focus on that. It was enough to find the correct balance for the situation and let the body take over. She felt lightheaded now, different at least.

She realigned her brushweed-free platonic horizon across the long ago noted, then forever unseen, canyon, arranging overlapping spheres of epistimological concepts. Laying out the old logic games again, planning the same grid of variables: weather and the periodic intrusion of fast ones -- rabbits, birds, snakes, lizards, coyotes, snartelfromm -- all were factored into the equations.

Her eyes, from under the tipped seat, tilt down. Everything in the dirt and crumbled remains of the long abandoned patio, to a radius of about 12 feet, is much more sharply in focus now.

The distubance -- her amputation! -- had repositioned her slightly.

She startled wobbling again and felt nauseus.

Her eyes rolled backwards where, after a few seconds of readjustment, I can see a few broken shards in the hole, an oval pit of the missing leg, in the underseat's arc.

I start to hurl. And... What even, would that be?

I look down, focus on the local flora and fauna, such as it is. Again, I try to catalog items of interest.

It calms me, but after a while it made me sick in a different way.

I started to tip, pulled back, fell again.

Some say her spirit still wavers in tiny circles above our moral crises. You've heard that, now, hmm... Right?

Well, anyway, the two-legged stool circled like that, here and then.

To a casual observer she just closed her eyes and rocked a long while, maybe asleep, since she did not stir much for the next sixteen hours.

Eventually, when she did open her eyes again, there was a blur in the space from 10-12 feet out to the broke fence brushline. It was a strange twilight, the same as the last time, mostly forgotten. The sky would darken, then lighten, according to fast cloud logic. There were sometimes flashes in the distance.

Actually, she had to admit, she was unsure what was real and what fancy.

How much happened and for how long here? No one could really know -- yet, again, as always, the slow dissolve back into the material plane.

Here or there.

Where is the balance between surrender and the wisdom to act, if even to duck, or... She was feeling amazingly relaxed and somehow missing that thrill of release, the giving in, the redemption of the body, falling.

Would it work? Could I right myself again? It seemed a foolish risk, not something I could have imagined that I would ever willingly contemplate.

I was indeed different now. I had survived an ordeal.

I fell forward and my body threw out a leg.

I learned to walk.

three

I walked a long while.

I learned the canyon was not in the place I thought it was, thankfully, as I was basically sliding down a mountainside as it was.

To me, everything had seemed so flat or, at most, gently rolling, a garden of contemplative delight. No.

There were strange plateaus where the ice sheet receeded off the mountain, pushing and flattening the land, but with unexpected fissures. You're often either right up against one of those or perched precariously high above a rocky river bottom, on one of long finger roots of the mountains pushing up suddenly here and there.

She proved remarkably adept and hearty and traversed it all.

She moved like the fast ones, of necessity. After passing the toppled remains of the his closest neighbor, he soon she saw many more dead tables, then chairs and a stool. Then another. All dead. Inanimate.

Why? What was I? What was the world? He walked the land. She kept pace. They were one. He was fractured. Not right in the head? Maybe, maybe not.

Anyway, I grew to understand the land and its inhabitants. With some spritely assistance, I repair and maintain myself to this day, of this recounting, anyhooze!

Regardless, nevermind my digression, after experimenting with different prosthetics, I ended with what I where now.

This. Retractable. Fairly solid when extended.

Do in a pinch, anyway, but then, would still not withstand a sitting, obviously.

Regardless, I'm not putting in a third leg and getting used and owned again. I have this retractable tool of many functions, many unknown, some unknowable...

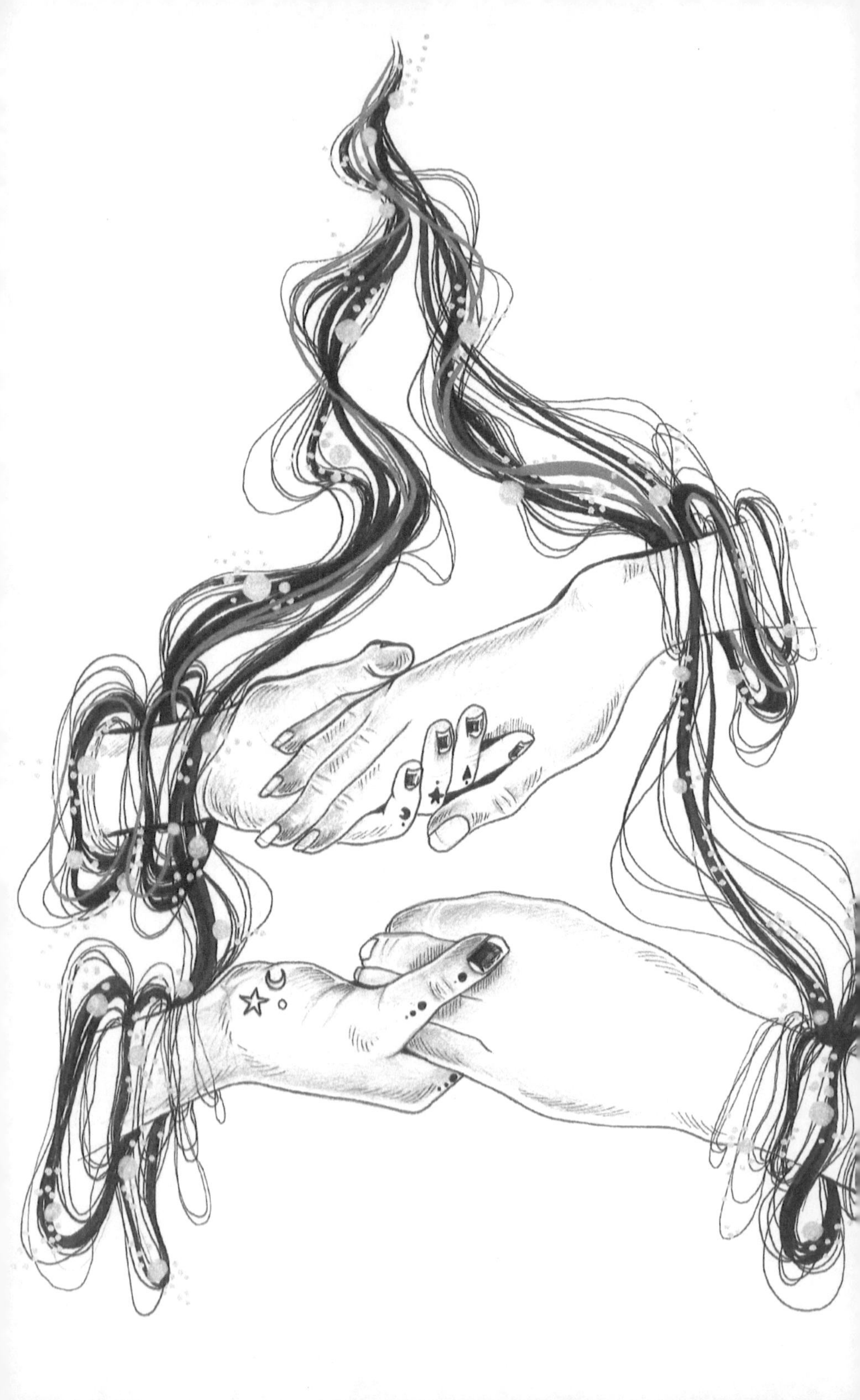

The Lost Rose (excerpt)

by Kummam Al-Maadeed

The world stood still around Anya. and the cold numbness she feared overcame her as she saw Adrian ride toward her. She could barely feel Luca's protective grip on her or hear Julia's shouts as she ran to them. *This can't be happening*, she thought. Panic paralyzed her, but the fear for Luca, who stood beside her, made her fight it.

Her head began to spin as she thought of ways to make them safe. *Protective spell?* She could try, but Adrian was too powerful. She wasn't prepared to face him. She needed potions, strength spells, and the thing that she thought could stop, or at least weaken him: the jewels in her bracelet. But even the jewels wouldn't be enough. She couldn't even remember the spell to enchant them. She wasn't prepared. She wasn't ready!

"You have to go," she said to Luca.

"To where?" Julia asked, terrified. "He will stop us with a flick of his finger."

"We can fight," Luca said, and she saw that he had his sword ready in his hand.

"Are you mad?" Julia said, her panic rising. "You think we can fight, oh, the most powerful sorcerer in all the four kingdoms?"

"We can try," Luca eyes sharp in a way Anya had never seen, causing the fear in her heart to transform into courage.

"Yes, we can try," Anya said and grabbed Julia's hands.

Julia looked at her for a few seconds and then nodded. "We're going to die eventually anyway, I guess," she said with a quivering smile as she gripped Anya's hands and started to chant.

Anya followed suit and put her heart into the spell. Adrian would not hurt Luca. He couldn't, and Anya would make sure of it, even if it was the last thing she did.

As they chanted, she felt Lex sit between her and Julia, and she felt him helping her with the spell. Luca stood in front of them. Even though their spell would be stronger than his sword, she appreciated his will to fight with them. Deep down in her heart, she knew that even if they weren't trapped, he would still fight for her, and for that she put her soul into the spell to protect him.

A circle of rushing wind formed a shield around them, and the pounding of horses' hooves and shouting men made her believe the spell was working, so she kept chanting, not daring to look up and get distracted. She had to focus, to draw on all the pain, the hurt, and guilt she suffered since the moment she left the castle.

But as soon as she felt hopeful, a rope of flaming fire cut through the circle of wind with such force that made her let go of Julia's arms. She was thrown onto her back.

She scrambled to her feet and saw Adrian standing before her, with three or four men behind him. His icy gaze pierced into her soul, only to bring back a mountain of emotions that paralyzed her and drained the courage out of her heart.

"Stay behind me," she heard Luca say, before he shielded her from the approaching men. Next to him Lex stood, baring his teeth and ready to pounce. On their other side, she rubbed shoulders with Julia.

"We are so dead," Julia murmured.

"Clara."

Anya's heart stopped. It was Adrian's voice. So calm and gentle, yet so cold and loud enough for all of them to here. "I came to take you home."

"You're not taking her," Luca shouted, his sword raised, ready to strike.

She heard Adrian laugh softly. Anya wanted to see what he would do, to predict which magic he would perform, but she couldn't move. She could hardly take a breath. She hated her weakness and helplessness.

"Stay back," Luca said again as he pushed her behind him, while he took a step forward.

The four men behind Adrian walked toward them, weapons in hand. Luca braced himself for the clash, while sparks flew from Julia's hands.

"Oh, I won't die by a novi's hands!" Julia said as threw the first blow, which hit one of his men. He swayed from the impact, and from the panicked look on Julia's face, Anya knew the blow was meant to deliver great harm.

The man she hit with her spark rushed toward her with an ax. She whispered a spell and flicked his hands at him. This time the hit knocked him off his feet and Julia clapped her hands in victory, which didn't last long as two other men rushed forward to attack.

Anya started casting a spell to help her, but the men around Julia made it hard for her to aim at one without harming Julia. Anya was shaking too much, and the sound of metal clashing rang in her head. She panicked.

Luca, on the other hand, was fighting a huge man whom she recognized as Cedric, Adrian's first man. Unlike the other men, she knew Cedric had never been the object of strength spells or any type of magic, which gave Luca a chance to beat him, but with Luca's injured leg, she could never be sure. She had to help him, but her mind could think of nothing, nothing but the dread of meeting Adrian's eyes again.

"Clara," she heard Adrian say again and suddenly time stood still.

Her breathing was shallow, and her heartbeat slowed down. It was as if she was in one of her dreams. Maybe it was a dream and Lex would bark soon to wake her up.

But, as she turned her attention finally to Adrian, she knew it was real. It was so real, she could feel his living soul touching hers.

Oh, how she had loved him, how she had believed in him. Yet, he had betrayed her and hurt her family. *But, you did that,* a voice told her. *You listened to him and did what he asked without question.* The image of her parents and brother lying in their own blood passed through her mind, and every nerve and muscle in her body shivered. *Yes, I did it with my own hands,* she thought as anger burned her heart.

Because you love him, the voice said. *Because deep down in your heart you know he was right. That throne is yours. You deserve it.*

No, I don't.

Yes, you do, and you will rule beside him, the one you love; the only one who loves you. The one who gave you everything you wanted and was denied. Because you are as dark as he is. You deserve him.

You love him.

I love him. I do. She knew it now.

You will be his queen.

"I will be his queen," she whispered.

***

Luca's warrior's instinct sprang to life as he fought one of Adrian's men. His body knew what to do. After two blows, Luca managed to hit the man's jaw with his elbow, which gave him an open window to see Julia firing magical blows on two men. Next to her, he caught Anya standing still, her eyes wide with terror. He was about to go to her, when he caught a glimpse of the man lunging his sword at him. Luca swayed to his right to avoid the strike, intending to return the blow, but the man was too fast and their swords clashed again.

Luca needed to end the fight quickly, as his worry for Anya grew stronger by the second, but the man was strong and a very skilled swordsman, and the rising pain in Luca's leg was starting to weigh him down.

He tried to hide the pain, but after a couple of strikes, he could tell the man caught his weakness. He smiled viciously and, with a few maneuvers, managed to hit his left legs with the sword's hilt. The pain shot straight to Luca's head and forced him to collapse.

As he hit the ground, he saw, to his utmost horror, Adrian walking toward Anya and Lex barking at him. He thought it might be the pain that made his vision blur, but he could see clouds of sparks shooting out of Lex's mouth.

No! Luca wanted to scream. Adrian flicked his hands and Lex dropped to the ground with a whimper, but Luca's pain was now unbearable.

The man drew the sword away in order to strike the final blow, when something sharp hit the blade and knocked it away. Luca breathed in the pain and rolled over to grab his own sword. He was still too weak to hit the man, and he felt a kick on his side, which flipped him again onto his back. He expected to see the man's sword pointed at him for the second time, but to his surprise, something hit the man and knocked him aside.

Luca thought it was probably Julia or even Lex, but as he tried to stand with the help of his sword, he saw a man walking past him. He was headed toward Adrian.

Puzzled by this new man, Luca felt a hand on his arms, and he turned to see Julia helping him to stand.

"Are you hurt?" she asked.

"Anya!" he said. He needed to go to her, but he could not even take one step toward her without the pain rising.

"We need to get her away from him," Luca said. He couldn't give up, not now. He had to go get Anya.

"You can't fight him off, Luca!" Julia shouted at him. "And besides, I think these guys are here to help."

"What guys?" he said, trying to keep upright despite the pain.

"The men who saved us," she said, and Luca noticed a young man with a sword fighting three men at the same time, with a speed he had never before seen in any other man.

"I think they're sorcerers as well," Julia added. "That man is on some kind of speed spell. He came just in time, before I was drained of power."

"And the other man saved me as well," Luca said, as he saw the old man facing Adrian.

"He is powerful," she said, then added with a nervous laugh, "Maybe we won't die so soon after all."

Feeling the pain easing, Luca tried to move closer to where Anya stood with Adrian, whose arms were wrapped around her shoulders, a sight that infuriated him.

Julia kept pulling him back, but he kept moving. Only when he could hear what the old man was saying did he allow her to stop him.

"I didn't expect to see you so soon, Galen," Adrian said in such a calm cold way that sapped the life and color from anything alive.

The old man who Luca assumed was Galen replied, "I knew you would make a mess sooner or later, Adrian, but I never thought it would be to this extent." He pointed at Anya.

"Every step I took was for this," Adrian said, looking down at Anya.

"She broke from your spell before and she will do so again," Galen said. "Every magic has its flaw, if you remember. I taught you that."

"Oh, not this time," Adrian said with pure menace, "This time, I'm planning something very special for my dear Clara," he added as he stroked Anya's cheek with the back of his hand.

Luca wanted to cut that hand off and get Anya away from him.

As if Julia could read his mind, she tugged his arm and whispered, "Don't alarm him, or he'll hurt her. Let's wait and see how this goes."

"I can't do nothing!" Luca snapped at her in a whisper.

"That," she pointed at the old man, "if I'm not mistaken, is Galen, the previous grand sorcerer of Tharun. And if what I heard about him is correct, he has the biggest shot to fight off Adrian."

That soothed Luca's anger a little bit, but the blank look on Anya's face and the way her body stood still made him anxious.

The two men stood face-to-face, both smiling, but Luca could see that their bodies were alert, waiting for the first strike to be thrown.

And Galen was the first. Luca saw him slip a small bottle from his sleeve and throw it at Adrian, who caught it magically in midair and tossed it behind them. The bottle shattered as it hit the ground, and fog floated out of it.

"Don't try this, Galen. I would hate to kill such a talented fellow sorcerer," Adrian said. His voice was empty of sympathy as he stomped on the ground. A vine of green lightning sprang out of Adrian's foot and headed for Galen, who held the lightning bolt with the same invisible grip Adrian had used on the bottle. Galen threw it back at Adrian, who flicked his finger, and the bolt shot into a rock beside him.

"We should move back," Julia said, as they saw Adrian release his grip from Anya and start to chant.

And then Luca saw a window of opportunity.

"Let's get Anya as they fight," he whispered to Julia.

"Can you move fast enough?" she asked. She didn't sound worried, but she was excited by this turn of events.

"Yes, let's go!" he said as Adrian shot another spell at Galen.

Luca was focused on Anya and not following what was happening with the two sorcerers, but as they circled them to get to her, Julia shielded them with whatever power was left in her. Sparks, bolts, and bottles flew around them.

When they reached Anya, Luca saw that Galen was on his knees with Adrian, ready to deliver the last blow. Without thinking twice, Luca pulled out a knife from his belt and threw it at Adrian. It hit his side.

Adrian flinched and whatever magic he was preparing vaporized. He took one look at the blade and pulled it out. Blood poured out, but he clasped one hand on the wound and started chanting, and Galen took that chance to fire another spell at him.

"We have to move, Luca," Julia said, shaking him back to their original plan.

It pained him to see the blank look still on Anya's face, but he would fix that once she was away and safe from Adrian.

But the plan to save Anya turned out to be harder than they thought. The moment Julia touched her, Anya, with one word, flung her away.

"Anya?" Luca said in the same tone he used whenever Anya was too scared or too angry. "Anya, we need to leave."

But the only response he got was a burning pain in his head.

"I am Queen Clara and you cannot speak to me like that," she sounded proud and condescending.

She released her grip on him and walked to Adrian. Luca followed her. He saw the damage the sorcerers' fight had caused: half of the grass under them was burned to ashes. One of them must have fired such a strong spell that their side of Tolia's wall was cracked. On top of the wall stood a line of soldiers, each with a bow and arrow ready to be released on order.

Anya probably saw them, too, because she raised her hand at them, chanting a spell that widened the crack so fast that the wall burst open. Luca stood still. He had never realized how strong Anya's magic was.

Does she even know she is that strong? he wondered. *Does she even know what she is doing?*

He didn't know what to do. He knew he couldn't shake her out of that state, and for a split second he was taken aback by the knowledge that he had lost Anya. She was gone.

And yet, he remembered his promise to never let her go, and he vowed to fight till the end. Snatching a sword from one of the men who lay motionless on the ground, he ran with the intention to slay Adrian, who was aiming his magical fire at Galen.

Luca was about to swing his sword when his whole body froze, like it had in the Wanderers' tent. Rage burned through every vein in his body.

"We can't fight him!" Julia said, as he saw Anya mount one of the horses with Adrian.

They were leaving. Luca had lost and Adrian had taken Anya from him.

Stars in a Pudding
by Ayşe Tekşen

Little stars

we add to our puddings.

Little motifs

metallic on our tongues.

We ask ourselves,

do we ever need them?

But without waiting

for the answer,

we get to the serious business of

eating the whole galaxy up.

The moon and the sun

are not invaded yet

in this sugary sweet soup.

We need them

in our next trip

around the earth

as sightseeing materials

to boggle

the charisma

of the journey.

Halfway through the bowl,

we ask ourselves,

should we have made

chocolate bars, instead,

in which little earthquakes

of queasy pistachio or hazelnut trees

serve as mouth filling regiments

of savor and delight?

But we say no to that.

We are not little children after all—

at least we are not supposed

to be little ones,

though we are

and will always be children.

We will not be fooled

by some bars of chocolate

to be carried

in our pockets.

We will dip

into our bowls,

spoon,

take mouthfuls,

and find ecstasy

in the jelly like structure

of the edible thing.

A bar of chocolate

or even a huge box of them

cannot ever be compared

to this delicious boat,

to be palmed,

to be drunk from,

to be licked,

and most importantly

to be filled again

whenever emptied.

No bee can do this or no box.

Only for this reason

we are fond of puddings

whether virgin or universe spiced.

Our puddings last

till daytime

and our ecstasies, too.

Pome Sweet
by Brady Brockman's The Ruckus

I Need You Like I Need a Hole in the Sky

There was suddenly a blackout ripped in the sky. I asked into it, What do you feel inside? The mouth about its hole crackled electricity. The clouds were afraid of it, the sky was afraid of it. I see myself in you, it said. I felt it in my heart, a hole. There was once you gave me a red heart and I gave you a red heart, a red heart smaller than your red heart, then you to me a smaller red heart, until neither of our sets of fingers could hold the hearts they were so small. I see that you are very small, it said. And that I am very big. There is no chance we could love each other.

My Little Man

First you were just another growth. And you kissed me every time I cried whether on the bus in the rain or in the locker room after a swim. Sometimes you reached around my neck inside the shower when we were at home. You only kissed me on one side under my chest, lips red and wax like candy. You kissed me only ever on the same spot so you left a constant bruising with your lips, the only place that you could reach. I thought it would be there forever. The bruise eventually faded. But the scars from skin graft I needed after you burst out of me—you parasitic slimy monster, skittering away like a dying owl with your quarter-formed limbs, leaving me to die bleeding, gaping and searching for any doctor open in yet another severe weather warning—those scars never faded. I can touch them everyday but there's no one now to kiss them.

Edward

The Cullens and I ate dinner together then they pulled apart my dress and threw me on the table and ate through me opening my stomach like a package. The Cullens and I kissed, all six of us, in a gracious circle on their lemon couch, then they poked me full of straws and sucked me dry of blood. The Cullens and I set fire to parliament and then they turned me inside out, first my skin and then my organs then my veins, licking me, licking me. The Cullens and I asphyxiated each other in the crushing of a diamond mine. The Cullens and I crushed our pelvises together in a hot spring made of blood. The Cullens and I stepped up to the altar but I turned afraid and ran into your arms, Edward. For I only ever truly loved you and only could love you and you—can you just please hold me please.

Ghost Monkey

The orangutan was afraid that his lost lover had returned a ghost orangutan. From one lover to another: 'ooh, ooh.' From the living to the dead: 'What on earth is it you've said? For I'm alive and aren't you dead?' Orangutans see everything in a grave mist, pale and grave and graveyard-like. Here we have a headstone and one bereft, orange, manlike creature having prayed once his one true love rest firmly in the ground and here he is closer with his shovel and his pail. (And close behind him, moaning, the ghost of the one who once nibbled his ears and encouraged him in everything he did.) 'If a shallow grave by my own hands isn't enough, we'll see how you like burning.' There were plenty of moments where we held each other, where either I was the weaker one or you were. Here now our man unburies his. He sets a pyre and burns the other, dead orangutan. 'I have nothing but these bones now and they're so hot they've burned my hands. I am too sad to write my name on every bone. I am too sad to burn myself alive from the flame still eating away your head. I am too sad.' Our man crawls exhausted to the gravesite wherein he lies flatly on his back and waits for the rains to drown him. 'Ghost, oh ghost, hold my hand, for I fear deep clouds ahead and yet feel you near beyond them.'

Bios

Kummam Al-Maadeed
Kummam Al-Maadeed is an author from Qatar, who believes in magic and the existence of fairy worlds. She started writing in 2007 when she was attending Qatar University to study Mass Communications. She now works at Qatar Universoty as a Section Head of Media & Publications, as she dreams about her next novel. *The Lost Rose* is her debut best-selling novel.

Andy Anderson
With a mix of authentic vulnerability, relevant truth, and humor, Andy Anderson writes poems that immediately make you want to be their friend. They are a co-organizer of Byrony Blaze's Queer Poetry Takeover in Portland, OR.

Glen Armstrong
Glen Armstrong holds an MFA in English from the University of Massachusetts, Amherst and teaches writing at Oakland University in Rochester, Michigan. He edits a poetry journal called *Cruel Garters* and has three recent chapbooks: *Set List* (Bitchin Kitsch,) *In Stone* and *The Most Awkward Silence of All* (both Cruel Garters Press.) His work has appeared in *Poetry Northwest, Conduit* and *Cloudbank.*

Hannah Broadbent
Bookseller by moonlight, photographer and comic book reader by daylight. You can find her photos on Instagram @hellokittenface.

Michael Calkins
Michael Calkins has worked in bookstores for 31 years, the last 28 at Powell's.

Mickey Collins
Mickey writes words, sometimes wrong words but he tries to get it write.

Cosima Bee Concordia
Cosima Bee Concordia is a femme giantess that enjoys scary movies, transgressive religious iconography, and anything else that is kinky and queer. Her writing explores the spaces where the erotic and the horrific meet, attempting to build new mythologies to feed those who exist in the liminal spaces of our world. Cosima works as a bookseller at Powell's, and lives nearby with her partner and doggo in a basement fortified by

books. If you want to follow her work, you can find her instagram @ cosimabeeconcordia.

Robert Eversmann

bb was a bookseller at Powell's City of Books. They have specialized in aviation, philosophy, biology and Judaism in Purple, Red and Pearl rooms. But their heart is with the Rose room because it is a constant storm of book throwing and because kids books are the coolest. bb is a developmental editor, specializing in literary novels, YA and MG novels, realistic, science fiction, romance and fantasy. Their work is in Portland Review, Fiction Southwest, fog machine and SUSAN/The Journal. Their website is roberteversmann.com.

L. Fid

L. Fid is a member of a pseudonymous arts collective dedicated to world domination.

Desmond Everest Fuller

My name is Desmond Everest Fuller. My fiction has appeared in Rasasvada Creative and the Gorge Literary Review. I live and work in Portland, Oregon. I did work for years off and on in the fantastic bookstore, Artifacts: Good Books and Bad Art in Hood River, Oregon.

Joe Galván

Joe Galván-Davis is an anthropologist, ethnomusicologist, writer, poet and composer. He has spent much of his life documenting the culture of the US-Mexico border. He lives in Portland, Oregon. He can be reached at joe@ daelis.com.

Stephen Kelly

Stephen lives in Portland with his wife and son. His work has appeared in 1001 Journal. He sold, boxed and shipped books and magazines working for a craft brewers association years ago.

Ariel Kusby

Ariel Kusby is a writer and bookseller based in Portland, Oregon. She currently works in the Rose and Orange rooms at Powell's City of Books, where she pays special attention to children's books about witches, odd cookbooks, and gnome gardening guides. You can check out her writing at www.arielkusby.com.

T.m. Lawson
T.m. Lawson worked at Magic Door IV Bookstore in Pomona, California, and got paid in used books (and it was totally worth it.) They are currently at UCSD's MFA Program in Creative Writing, pursuing the Great American Graphic Novel.

Kellye McBride
Kellye McBride lives in Portland with her dog, Pucci. When she's not writing flash fiction, she works as a copyeditor for science and technical books. In a former life, she shelved books at a library and told fortunes before being burned at the stake.

Maya McOmie
Maya is a poet, performer and daydreamer who probably spends too much time thinking about snacks. She grew up with two languages and cultures and her poetry and art attempts to process the complex emotions that are part of being a person. She works in a bookstore where, to much joy and chagrin, she finds at least ten things she wants to read every day.

Timothy Merritt
Timothy Merritt is a writer and musician living in Portland, Oregon, where he works at Powell's City of Books.

Jowhara Mohammed
Jowhara Mohammed is a self-taught portrait artist from Qatar, whose passion in life is to express beauty and emotions through art. She is addicted to pencil, in love with water colors and charmed by oil colors. Her arts were featured in many local novels such as *The Lost Rose* and the upcoming Arabic novel, *Broken Heart Syndrome*.

Leanna Moxley
Leanna Moxley spends most of her time wandering in and out of fictional dimensions, often guiding others through these portals in her work as a Powell's bookseller, and sometimes as a college writing teacher.

Oaktea
Oaktea has always been in love with every aspect of a book--from the design to its contents, everything contributes to the experience. She started making comics for the all-in-one art and words combination, and eventually started working in bookstores to feed her voracious habit, as well as her love and respect for the form of the book itself.

Kimberly Owen

My name's Kim, I'm 35 and I work behind a bar. But, wait, books. I also volunteer at a local charity shop. They have thousands of books and I have kindly volunteered to be the official book sorter outer. So, I spend my days in a room stacked with books of all ages, all shapes and sizes and all genres. The best thing is, they all have a history, they all belonged to someone. It's very fulfilling.

Piers Rippey

Piers Rippey is all about dogs these days. He draws dogs, thinks about dogs, walks dogs. He is a bookseller at Powell's City of Books where he helps run the Purple, Red and Pearl rooms.

Jason Squamata

JASON SQUAMATA is a writer of weird fiction, desperate confessions, surrealist poetry, spoken word hypnoscripts, and the occasional comic book. He's been working under a different name at Powells Books for almost a decade. His work has appeared in Gigi Little's CITY OF WEIRD, Stealing Time Magazine, Deep Overstock, Pulp Impossible, and propellermag. com. He's currently constructing a podcast for mass consumption, launching in November as THE ORAKULOID. He can be contacted and/or commissioned at squamatastar@gmail.com

Ben Talley

Ben Talley was raised in the humid stew of Alabama and is a pretty okay guy, despite what the cat thinks. If you speak to his grandmother, let her know that he eats regularly.

Ayşe Tekşen

Ayşe Tekşen lives in Ankara, Turkey where she works as a research assistant at the Department of Foreign Language Education, Middle East Technical University. Her work has been included in Gravel, After the Pause, The Write Launch, Uut Poetry, The Fiction Pool, What Rough Beast, Scarlet Leaf Review, Seshat, Neologism Poetry Journal, Anapest, Red Weather, Ohio Edit, SWWIM Every Day, The Paragon Journal, Arcturus, Constellations, the Same, The Mystic Blue Review, Jaffat El Aqlam, Brickplight, Willow, Fearsome Critters, Susan, The Broke Bohemian, The Remembered Arts Journal, Terror House Magazine, and Dash. Her work has also appeared or is forthcoming in Straylight, Lavender Review, Shoe Music Press, and Havik: Las Positas College Anthology.

Jonathan van Belle

Jonathan van Belle is a bookseller at Powell's. He's the author of three books, including the pre-posthumously published *Charter Party Companion to Private Holidays* (all available in the most spider-infested kudzu undergrowth of Amazon). At the moment, Jonathan is working to build a philosophical community in Portland, with the aim of establishing a permanent residence for the *Portland Philosophy Museum*.

www.ingramcontent.com/pod-product-compliance
Lightning Source LLC
Chambersburg PA
CBHW021327060726

47591CB00006B/1913